LONGMAN LITERATURE

DAZ 4 ZOE

Robert Swindells

Editor: Roy Blatchford

 LONGMAN

Longman Literature
Series editor: Roy Blatchford

Novels

Other titles in the Longman Literature series are listed on pages 194 and 195.

Contents

The writer on writing

by Robert Swindells

Them and us. Us and them. Create division within a society and before you know it those on one side of the line start hating those on the other side. It's inevitable. Doesn't matter where the line's drawn. It might divide rich from poor. Black from white. Male from female. Tall from short. The result's always the same: suspicion becoming fear becoming hatred leading to conflict.

It's happening today at a location near you. The law requires schools to test their pupils and publish the results so that league tables can be compiled, using crude statistics to divide schools into 'good' and 'bad'. Of course it's not that simple. Different schools have different problems, and some have more problems than others. Testing can't measure this. League tables can't reflect it. What they can do – what they are doing – is to create a division within society between those young people who have attended 'good' schools and those who, through no fault of their own, have attended 'bad' ones.

There's an element of self-fulfilling prophecy in the system because educated, articulate parents will be more successful than less educated, less articulate parents in getting their children into the school of their choice. Naturally they'll choose a 'good' one, and that school's test results will reflect its advantaged intake. Meanwhile the children of the less well educated will go to the 'bad' schools, whose results will reflect their intake.

I wrote **DAZ 4 ZOE** to try to show what might happen if such a system were carried to its logical conclusion. I leave it to my reader to decide whether I have succeeded, and whether the society I portray is the sort of thing we ought to be aiming at.

Introduction

The writer's background

Robert Swindells was born in 1939 on the eve of the Second World War (1939–1945). His childhood years were spent in and around Bradford, Yorkshire, and amongst his earliest memories is the arrival of parcels sent by his father away in Canada with the Royal Air Force. For these parcels contained sweets, sugar, coffee, chocolate – a range of 'goodies' that were strictly rationed in wartime England.

Another vivid memory is how he used to conjure up in his mind strange and curious characters based on snippets of adult conversation. At the same time he was becoming an avid reader; books became an escape route for him, a way out of a busy house and an ordinary life. He recalls:

> I was ten when the last of my brothers was born. There were six of us now, and my parents were having a hard time providing for us all. Dad's job as a travelling salesman provided a fluctuating income – sometimes we were all right, sometimes not. He was away a lot, too, and I guess Mum resented his leaving her to cope with us kids alone – she'd had enough of that in the war. Anyway, the strain began to cause rows between them which distressed me greatly.

> I retreated even further into my fantasy world, reading all day when I wasn't in school and often, with aid of a flashlight, far into the night. I began making up stories too, inside my head. I'd play these stories back endlessly on my long walks to and from school, and at night in my bed. It was better than dwelling on the ceaseless bickering, the thousand shabby little economies of home. Better than reality.

> Something About the Author Autobiography Series, vol. 14

After failing the eleven-plus examination, the author went to a secondary modern school, where he encountered a gifted teacher of English. Mr Gledhill not only read but acted out for his pupils **Kidnapped**, **Treasure Island** and many more classic adventure novels. The power of story impressed itself on the young Swindells's mind. He has always remained indebted to Mr Gledhill for mesmerising his class and telling his pupils that they could be anything they wanted -- 'all we had to do was believe'.

Leaving school at fifteen, the author had a range of jobs in factories, a newspaper office, and a three-year spell in the RAF. At the age of thirty he decided to take examinations in order to go to college, and it was while there that he wrote his first novel. In fact he wrote that children's novel as a kind of examination thesis in his third and final year, and was then quite amazed to find that his tutor suggested it deserved to be published. And it was, by Brockhampton Press in 1973, under the title **When Darkness Comes**.

Following some eight years as a part-time teacher and part-time writer, Robert Swindells decided in 1980 to make writing his full-time career. Looking back on his very varied life to date, he recalls, honestly and movingly:

> I've neither worked particularly hard nor lived a particularly virtuous life and yet I have everything I need: everything I ever truly wanted. Why? How do these things happen?

> Partly of course it's being born in the right place. Pop out of the womb in most parts of Ethiopia, Bangladesh or Guatemala and there's little chance you'll realise even a fraction of your potential, no matter how hard you try.

> Partly it's the talents you're born with. Everybody's good at something. It's just that some talents are more useful than others, some are of no use at all, and some just get you into trouble.

> Mostly though, it's other people. Parents. Teachers. An understanding employer along the way. A rich old uncle. Some we remember with gratitude and affection. Most we don't remember at all, or never even knew, so that we're tempted to think of ourselves as self-made men, when in truth there's

*no such thing. George Eliot said it a long time ago, in **Middlemarch**: '... that things are not as ill with you and me as they might have been, is half owing to the number who lived faithfully a hidden life, and rest in unvisited tombs'.*

I hope you can hear me, Mum. You, and all the others, because I want to say thanks. I mean it. It's been fantastic, and it never would have happened without you.

Something About the Author Autobiography Series, vol. 14

The writer's ideas

In common with probably all writers, Swindells's own early experiences have shaped much of his fiction. Clearly, his escape into books at an early age has been a significant corner-stone in his life as a writer. He acknowledges that Enid Blyton was a strong influence on him: 'I liked the sort of story where children went off on their own and there were no adults. Many of my books are like that now. She may not have made a writer out of me, but she made a reader out of me. My primary aim is to convince young people that reading for pleasure is a worthwhile thing to do.'

There is also little doubt that the author's own sense of failure at not passing the eleven-plus examination has influenced him. His father hit him for his failure and began to mock his son's constant reading, frequently saying that he'd never amount to much. Swindells experienced a 'helpless rage' at this and determined to better himself.

But the scars of failure at eleven for the author (and for many millions of children who did not go to grammar school) were deep; what the author has to say in 'The writer on writing' section (page iv) about divided schools today has its roots in his own childhood in the 1950s.

Robert Swindells's interest in and concern for the way society has changed and developed during his lifetime surface strongly in two of his other novels. He has been a long-term activist with the antinuclear movement and in 1987 was imprisoned for seven days for his part in a CND (Campaign for Nuclear Disarmament) non-violent direct action. The novel *Brother in the Land* presents an appalling picture of those who survive a nuclear bomb; its story will convince anyone that such weapons of mass destruction are evil.

More recently, the author has turned his attention to the number of young people he has seen sleeping rough in doorways in London. He was especially angry at a politician who had the gall to say that 'the homeless are the sort of people you step on when coming out of the opera'. The novel *Stone Cold* offers a brutal picture of life on the streets of London in the 1990s, seen through the eyes of the young homeless.

One particular feature of *Stone Cold* is its clever and disturbing use of a double narrator, so that we watch through the eyes of two different characters. Swindells suggests that he likes this device because it allows him 'to show how an event or situation may be perceived differently depending on the observer's viewpoint'. And so it is with Daz and Zoe: their alternating 'voices' guide us through the action.

DAZ 4 ZOE

DAZ 4 ZOE – note the writer's deliberate use of capital letters – was first published in 1990 and, like *Stone Cold*, is a powerful picture of decaying urban life. On page 2 of the novel the author writes:

> *The rest of this book is fiction but it could come true, and we wouldn't like it if it did. You'll see what I mean when you've read it. It could come true, but it won't if we're together. All of us.*
>
> *There's no reason why we shouldn't be.*

With this note of warning, Robert Swindells is following in the footsteps of many great writers before him who have seen it as

INTRODUCTION

their responsibility both to entertain and to educate their readers. In the nineteenth century, the novelist Charles Dickens used such novels as **Oliver Twist** and **Hard Times** to bring to the attention of the general public and politicians the desperate poverty of many families living in Victorian London.

Fifty years later, Wilfred Owen wrote poems about the 1914–18 World War that he hoped would alert future generations to the terrifying waste of lives that war brings – and therefore help to prevent a repetition of his generation's mistakes. Then in the 1940s it was George Orwell's turn to offer warnings to his readers – in **Animal Farm** and **1984** – about the way power corrupts and can lead to leaders wickedly controlling the lives and minds of those they rule over.

What makes **DAZ 4 ZOE** gripping reading is that its setting, sometime in the future – when exactly we are left to guess – is worryingly believable. We are not cast into a sci-fi future world of robots and aliens, merely projected forward into a divided city that, if we look over our shoulders, just could be Manchester, Glasgow or Portsmouth in fifty years time. Or could it?

Grandma in the novel writes 'we are members one of another'. Swindells – an author and a man who believes that tolerance and cooperation *can* win over brutality and injustice – seems to be drawing the reader towards the conclusion that young people like Daz and Zoe do not have to be members of a divided generation. But he has also noted in a recent interview:

> My message to my readers is 'No, everything's not all right. You're about to enter the adult world and you've got work to do if that world is ever to know peace and justice.'

Roy Blatchford, *Everything's Not All Right* (Stanley Thornes), 1996

Reading Log

The study programme at the back of this book provides many ideas and activities for *after* you have read the novel. However, you are likely to give a better response to the text if you make some notes as you read. Those who assess your coursework assignments or examination answers are looking for evidence of a personal response to literature; to do well, this should be supported by some close analysis and reference to detail.

Keeping notes as you read should help you to provide this, as well as to keep track of events in the plot, characters and relationships and the time-scheme of the novel. When you are reading, stop every so often and use the following prompt questions and suggestions to note down key points and details.

Plot

- What have been the main developments in the plot? Note down exactly where they occur.
- How has the author 'moved the story on' – for example, by introducing a new character or by a change of setting?
- Is there more than one storyline?
- How do you expect the plot/s to develop? As you read on, consider whether you predicted accurately or whether there have been some surprises.

Characters

- What are your initial impressions of the main character/s? Are these impressions confirmed or altered as you read? How?

- Do any of the main characters change or develop through the novel? How and why?

- How are you responding to individual characters? In particular, are you aware that you are identifying or sympathising with one of them? Are you conscious of ways in which the author is making or encouraging you to do this, for example by focusing on his/her point of view, or by providing insights into his/her thoughts and feelings?

Setting

The setting of a novel is the place and time in which the events happen. Sometimes the setting involves a particular community or culture. It can often make an important contribution to the prevailing atmosphere of the work.

- How well does the writer help you to visualise the setting? Make a note of any passages of description which you think are particularly effective in creating a vivid sense of place and time.

- Does the setting seem to be just a background against which the action takes place, for example because it is concerned with historical events?

Themes

The themes of a work of literature are the broad ideas or aspects of experiences which it is about. There are some themes – love, death, war, politics, religion, the environment – which writers have explored throughout the centuries.

- What theme or themes seem to be emerging in the novel?

- How is the theme developed? For example, do different characters represent different attitudes or beliefs?

- Does it seem that the writer wants to express his/her attitude to a theme to raise questions, or just to make the reader reflect on it?

Style

- Is the story told by a narrator who is also a character in the novel, referring to him/herself as 'I' (first-person narrative), or is the narrator anonymous and detached from the action (third-person narrative)?
- How does this affect the novel? For example, does a third-person narrator tell you what characters are thinking and feeling (known as an omniscient narrator) or comment directly on characters and/or events?
- Note down any interesting or striking use of language, such as powerful words and images which evoke a sense of atmosphere. Include any recurring or similar images.
- What do you think of the dialogue? Do the 'voices' of the characters sound real and convincing? Make a note of any particular features of the language used in the dialogue, such as dialect, colloquialisms, slang or expletives (swearing).
- How is the dialogue used, for example to show characters and relationships, for humour, to explore theme?

Your personal response

- How are your feelings about the novel developing as you read? What have you enjoyed or admired most (or least) and why?
- Has the novel made you think about or influenced your views on its theme/s?

DAZ 4 ZOE

A TRUE STORY

Palm trees don't like the cold. That's why they don't occur naturally in England. You see them sometimes in seaside towns but they never look right. Ragged they are, with dead bits hanging down.

Old people occur naturally in England, but they don't like the cold, either. Some of them are ragged too, and there are probably dead bits only you don't see them.

Anyway, there was this winter. It was a really cold winter – one of the coldest on record – with hard frosts every night. It was so cold that old people started dying. Daren't have the fire on, see. Not with electricity the price it was. So they wrapped themselves up in blankets and sat shivering till they fell asleep and died, like lost explorers in the Arctic.

And there was this seaside town that had some palm trees. Now palm trees can't feel the cold, but it kills them just the same. It was killing these particular palm trees all right. Slowly but surely.

Until one day the man that looked after them – the Town Gardener, I suppose – had this brilliant idea. What he did was, he got a lot of electric blankets and some very long cables and he plugged the blankets in and ran them out on the long cables and wrapped them round the palm trees. It took several blankets to wrap each tree but when he switched on, the trees were really snug.

Every night the Town Gardener switched on, and night after night the electricity ran through the long cables, warming the blankets till the cold spell was over and the palm trees were saved.

Afterwards it was on telly and in the papers, how the palm trees were saved. What a good idea, people said. What a clever man. Everybody was really happy.

Well, no – not everybody. Some of the old folks – some of them that didn't die – moaned on about the waste of electricity, but you're going to get moaners whatever you do, and the moral of the story is you can't please everybody.

Or is it?

The rest of this book is fiction but it could come true, and we wouldn't like it if it did. You'll see what I mean when you've read it. It could come true, but it won't if we're together. All of us.

There's no reason why we shouldn't be.

DAZ

Daz thay call me. 2 years back wen I com 13 Del that's my brovver thay catch im raiding wiv the Dred. Top im don't thay, and im just gon 15.

2 lornorders com tel our mam, 1 wumin, 1 man, nor thay don't come til after thay dunnit neever. Our Mam been down a longtime fore then wiv the dulleye, and she just sort of stairs dont she, til thay go of, and its not til nite she crys.

She sez dont you never go of wiv no Dred, our Daz. No Mam, I sez, but I never crost my hart. Don't cownt less you crost yor hart, rite?

ZOE

Hi. I'm Zoe. Zoe May Askew. Or Zoe may not. (Joke!) I'm fourteen. My friend at school is Tabitha. Tabitha Flinders Wentworth for short. She's fourteen too. If the name seems familiar to you it's no big surprise. Her dad's Paul Wentworth of Wentworth and Lodge (Developments) PLC, the outfit that shoved up practically every residential estate in practically every suburb in England. You're bound to have seen their boards, plus their ads on T.V. He's into about a million other things too, Tabby says. Security. Roads. Power. He's into power all right. Chair of the Suburb Selectmen, Chair of Schools Management Committee, etcetera, etcetera, etcetera. Dog leaves a mess on the sidewalk, Paul Wentworth'll make himself Chair of it.

They're loaded. Well, you can imagine. They live in this gorgeous architect-designed house on Wentworth Drive. That's right – Wentworth Drive. He built the place and named it after himself, and why not?

I know what you're wondering. You're wondering how come Tabby Wentworth would bother with a scumbag like me, right? Sure you are. Well, my dad's an estate agent, see, and what estate agents do is they sell houses. You probably thought they sold cheeseburgers, but they sell houses. Wentworth builds 'em, Dad sells 'em. They're not friends, exactly, but they do a lot of business together and that's what it's all about, isn't it?

Well, no, as a matter of fact, it's not.

Listen. I want to tell you a story, only I've got to start at the beginning, right? And that's where Tabby Wentworth comes in. At the beginning. Because she started it. She started it because everything's boring and fourteen's a lousy age and chippying's about the only way you can get a bit of excitement around here. Chippying. If you've never heard of it, don't worry. You will. In fact you're going to know all about chippying real soon.

There's us and there's them, see? Subbies and Chippies. They don't call themselves Chippies, of course. I don't know what they call themselves, but I know they call us Subbies. That's because we live in the suburbs. We work and take showers and have nice houses. They don't. They hang out and live in crummy apartments and they don't even wash, for pete's sake. And they hate us. We're just ordinary, decent people, doing pretty much what people ought to do, but they hate us. Dad reckons it's envy. They envy us. They want our cars and our money and our nice houses, but they don't want our long years in school and they don't want to work. That's what Dad says, anyway. I don't know. I bet they're the same as everybody else, really, but I wouldn't say that to Dad. He says they get so many handouts they don't need to work. And if they want some money or a nice car, they just sneak into the nearest suburb and take it. That's why we have fences and lights and guards. That's how come we have to carry I.D. all the time, and why we keep moving if we go outside.

Say you have an aunt or a cousin or somebody living in a neighbouring suburb and you want to visit with them. What you have to do is get in the car, check the tank, hit the freeway with your foot down and go like the clappers till you're there. It's the only way. You stop out there – you just so much as slow down and they got you. They're watching all the time, see. All the time.

Why Chippies, I hear you ask. Why do we call them Chippies. Well, that's easy. It's their favourite food, chips. They practically live on them. Everybody knows that. It's a well-known fact. And that's where chippying comes from. It means going out and mixing with the Chippies.

What happens is, some kid gets fed up being cooped up. I mean all right – a suburb's a pretty nice place. I'm not saying that. But any place with a fence around'll get to you, eventually. So this kid gets ballsed off and he calls a couple of buddies and they get in the car and go. Not down the freeway, 'cause that only takes you to the next nice prison. No. They take one of the turnoffs the copcars use and cruise into town. I mean right down there where the streets are dark and dirty with high, crummy buildings and broken glass everywhere. Why? Because the one thing those dumb Chippies know how to do is have a good time.

They have these clubs. Not like our clubs. I'm not talking about squash clubs or health clubs or bridge clubs, and I'm not talking about youth clubs, either, with bands that play gospel half the time. No. These clubs're night-clubs. You know. Dim, smoky little joints with booze and dope and bands that really belt it out. All the stuff the Chippies knock off, stuff they lift in the suburbs or take from hi-jack trucks gets fenced in the clubs. You might have seen something similar in old movies, but unless you chippy you're never gonna see one for real.

And that's where the kids go. Round the clubs. And if you think that's safe you're crazy. It's not safe. In fact it's downright dangerous, but that's all part of the fun.

The reason it's dangerous is, two reasons. First, you've got money and they don't, and they know you have it, and there's a lot of them and only a few of you. And second, they hate you anyway 'cause you're a Subby and they'd as soon kill a Subby as look at him.

So yes, it's dangerous, but you've got one thing going for you and it's this. You're here to spend money. Cash money, and cash is scarcer than hen's teeth in Chippyville. They call it peanuts. They'll kill for it, but killing brings the cops and they'd rather get it some other way. You spend it, they got it. You have a good time spending it, you're gonna come back again. And again. And again. And even a dumb Chippy knows you don't kill the goose that lays the golden eggs. So, as long as you tread soft and don't go looking for trouble, you should be okay.

I say should be, because every now and then a Subby'll disappear while chippying. Sometimes a whole carful goes out and never comes back. They've probably run into a Dred squad, or some guy looking for a fight. You can never be sure, see, and that's where the kick is. Right down there where the butterflies play.

Anyway, I'm going to tell you what happened the night Tabby and me went out. The night it all began, only Daz wants to say a bit first. It will be a bit 'cause he doesn't write too good but I wish you could see him. Your knees'd go weak, he's so brilliant.

DAZ

Don't you never go of wiv no Dred our mam sez, but wot woud you do eh? How woud you feal if you was 1 of us.

We do wot we can rite. We do. You cant graft if ther is non and ther is non. And its not easy to get a barf neever. Not wivout water its not, and we dont hav water a lot of the time.

And thay sit up ther in veezavill, larfin and tellin each ovver how them Chippys never graft and them Chippys never wash and them Chippys do this and them Chippys do that and them Chippys do the ovver. Its alrite for them innit. They got graft. Water. Peanuts. Its alrite for them wiv all them fast motors and brand new doodys. They mite wel larf wiv ther hi fences and dazzlers and bouncers garding them and al that. i'd larf.

It'd be bad enuf if thay staid behind ther fences but thay dont. Not all ov them. Sum com owt at nite, Chippying. Thats wot thay call it – Chippying. Means coming down ahrend, clubbing. Thay got clubs. Posh clubs, but thay got to come snooping in ars dont thay, giving it the la-di-la and larfin. Thay got peanuts to buy the best booze and get of wiv ar wimmin. Were dirty and funny, rite. But not ar wimmin. Thats diffrent innit.

I hate Subbys. Hate them. Mister James up at the school sez a long time ago ther was no Subbys and fings

8

wasnt so bad. Then Brittan rite – Brittan won the fork lands and got grate and sum people got to be Subbys and sum dint and that was us. So wot i fink is, get rid of the Subbys and fings'll be better. Stands to reason dunnit.

And that's wot the Dreds all about. Killing Subbys. You cant join til 15 and now I am so watch out you basteds i'll show you topping our Del.

ZOE

It was a Friday, I remember that, because when Tabby mentioned going out I thought, well, at least I won't have to be up for school tomorrow.

I'm not saying that was my first thought. It wasn't. I'm not that cool. My first thought was What? Who? Me?

It was ten to nine and we were parking our bikes. I'm fitting my front wheel in the slot and thinking about nothing in particular and she says, 'Fancy coming out tonight?'

'Huh – where?'

'Out. O-U-T. You know – down town.'

'Chippying?' My voice is a sort of croak. I know kids Chippy but nobody ever asked me before. It's a bit of a shock.

'Sure, Chippying,' she says. 'What d'you think I meant?'

I looked at her. 'I didn't know you went out.'

'I don't tell you everything I do,' she says. 'And anyway I only went once before.'

'When?'

'Three weeks ago. Four of us, in Ned Volsted's car. There was Ned, Tim Bixby, Sara Fanshaw and me. It was brilliant.'

'Why didn't you tell me?'

She shrugs, doesn't answer. Instead she says 'You in, or not?'

'Who else is going?'

'Ned, Larry Turner and me. And you, of course.'

'I haven't said I'll come yet. What about Tim and Sara?'

'What about them?'

'Why aren't they going again?'

'How do I know? Busy, I guess.' She grins. 'Or chicken.'

'Why – did something happen? Something bad?'

She shakes her head. We're walking away from the bikes. 'Nothing happened. I told you – we had a great night. You in or out? I can get somebody else.'

'I don't like Larry Turner. He's a creep.'

'So?' She shoots me a dirty look. 'You don't have to marry the guy. Just sit in the same car is all.'

It was then I had the thought about not having to get up for school. I don't want to kid you – I was nervous. In fact I was scared. Also, I didn't know how I'd get away. What I'd tell my parents. I mean you can't say 'Oh, by the way, Dad, I'm off down town tonight with some of the kids. We thought we'd get drunk, do a little coke, maybe dance with some of them husky Chippy guys. Look for me around three a.m.'

A part of me was terrified, and yet I wanted to go. I did. I felt I should anyway, because Tabby asked me and maybe she'd cool off if I refused. Stop being my friend. I don't make friends easily and I don't think I could stand that. So I told myself I didn't have to get up for school tomorrow, and then I said okay, I was in.

And that's how it began.

We used my cousin as an alibi. That's really why Tabby invited me. I knew that. Last time they used Sara Fanshaw's sister but Sara wasn't coming this time. Tabby's nice and all, but she's a user if you know what I mean. My cousin Alice lives over in Fairlawn which

11

is the suburb next to ours. It's four miles. Alice and Jim have a big place with ponies on it and Tabby loves to ride. My mother has taken us over there a few times so there was no problem when I told my folks. When it was time I said 'See you' and walked out and Ned picked me up at the end of the street. Easy peasy.

Ned's eighteen. He's in the sixth form. He's off to university in the autumn and says he won't be back. He's lived in Silverdale all his life and he reckons eighteen years in Silverdale's enough for anybody. I don't know. Whatever he does he's going to end up living in some suburb, and I hear they're all the same.

We picked up Larry next. He's sixteen, which makes him two years older than Tabby and me. He's a weedy little guy with snaggle teeth and zits, but his dad's a Silverdale Selectman and he thinks that makes him a star.

Tabby was waiting on the corner. She got in the back with me. The city's south of Silverdale but we were supposed to be heading west for Fairlawn, so we cruised along Westgate and stopped at the barrier. Ned rolled down the window and we sat looking innocent as the bouncer on duty stuck his head in. Bouncer's Chippy for security guard.

'I.D.?' We passed him our cards. He flicked through them and handed them back.

'Destination?'

'Fairlawn.' Ned has this very open smile. 'We're off to ride ponies with Ms Wentworth's friends.

The smile cut no ice. 'I don't care if you're off to ride giraffes with Dracula's uncle, kid. Stay on the freeway and keep moving, right?'

'Right.'

'Got gas?'

'Yessir. Full tank.'

'Coming back tonight?'

'Ah-ha.'

'Time?'

Ned shrugged. 'Eleven. Eleven-thirty. Depends.'

'Use this gate so we can check you in.'

'Right.'

The guy nodded to his friend in the gatehouse, the pole went up and we were out, whooping and slapping one another on the back as Ned went up through the gears. We headed west till we were clear of Silverdale, then found a cop route going south.

DAZ

its 2 days after i com 15 i tork 2 Mick my mate. Wot do i do abowt joining Dred, i arst.

i fought you'd never arst, he sez. Mick's in already, see.

Well i'm arsting now, i sez.

See Cal, he sez. Cal'll put you strait.

Wears he hang owt, i arst. This is friday morning rite, and we're off up the school. i reckon its my last time cos i'm jacking it in wen i get in Dred. Our mam wont like it but that's how it gos. I can rite and reckon and Mister James sez i'd hav no chance in the Veeza-Teeza so wot's the point? The Veeza-Teeza's this exam, rite? Once a year exam. If you pass you get a veeza to go to Subby school. You do gud ther and Zap! you're a Subby. About 2 kids pass each year. If that many.

Once Mister James fought i mite go in 4 it but it dint workout. Aniway who wants to be a Subby when you can be a Dred?

Blue Moon, sez Mick. Tonite. Blue Moon's this club. Nite club. Bands and strippers and pool and that. Yor spos to be 16 but no 1 bovvers. i bin in lotsa times.

Wot's he luck like, i arst. Mick larfs. i'll be wiv you, he sez. i'll introdooce you. He sez this in a Subby-type voice. Introdooce. He's a bit of a pillock old Mick, but hes alrite.

Aniway that's how com i'm in the Blue Moon that nite when these Subby kids com in and screw me up. i mean 1 of them dos. i'll fill you in later, rite?

14

ZOE

I'd never seen a city before, except on telly. You see them sometimes on the news. Glimpses shot from fans or moving vehicles when there's been a big robbery or a riot. Fan's helicopter in Chippy talk. Helicopter has four syllables and they can't handle it. That's what Dad says, anyway.

You get these glimpses and you can see they're a mess. And that's how Rawhampton looked as we approached it. Derelict houses, some burned out. Cracks in the road with weeds poking through. Piles of brick and glass and cement everywhere, all smashed up. It was hard to imagine what it must've been like in the old days, with cars and crowds and big stores and a million lights, like cities you see in ancient movies. Gran says she remembers the city that way but it's hard to imagine.

Anyway, there we were, cruising in through the outskirts and it was like dusk and you couldn't see too well. None of the street lights was working and Ned had to slow right down to keep from ramming piles of trash or driving into a hole or something. There were holes everywhere. Deep ones, full of slimy water. Ned switched on the headlamps, but it was that weird time halfway between daylight and dark when headlamps aren't much help.

There didn't seem to be any people about at first. Just dogs. You hear about the dogs on telly, how they hunt in packs through the streets, killing Chippy kids and eating them. You might have heard this sick joke:

Why did the dog eat the Chippy?

'Cause he was its Pal.

Pal – geddit?

They weren't in packs, the ones we saw. They were loners, dashing across in front of us with their tails between their legs. Some were pretty big, though, and they were all thin, and you could easily imagine them going for you if you didn't have the car.

As we drove further in we passed through a so-called residential development – multi-storey apartment blocks scattered across a wilderness of long grass and overgrown pathways. Most of the blocks were doorless and glassless and there was rubbish everywhere. Cans and bottles, plastic bags, filthy mattresses, the skeletons of baby-buggies, you name it.

And people. People leaning in doorways, shuffling along broken paths, framed in unglazed windows. Ragged men with their hands in their pockets and stubble on their cheeks. Slag-bag women with greasy hair and shapeless legs. Thin kids with bare feet and vacant expressions, watching our car go by. I shivered, wondering how people could bear to live like this.

As we left the residential area behind and approached the old commercial centre, I began to wonder how the Chippies could possibly have anything to offer us which was worth the awful risk of being here. If you want to know the truth I was scared. I mean, I knew the city wasn't going to be Disneyland or anything. I knew that before I came. And everybody knows chippying's dangerous. They run videos on telly about seven hundred times a night, warning you. One of them shows a car with all four doors open and a shoe lying in the road. Just a shoe. But it was worse than I'd expected and that was because of the eyes. Chippy eyes. What they should do is, they should show a video of Chippies looking at the camera like they looked at us that night. That cold, dead look with something behind it like waiting.

I said to nobody in particular, 'These clubs. What're they like?'

Tabby tittered. 'Dark. They're dark.'

'And noisy,' said Larry, twisting his stringy neck to look around at us. 'Fantastically noisy.'

'They're usually full of smoke, too,' Ned added. 'Your eyes start streaming after a bit.'

'So what's good about them?' I pursued. 'I mean, it seems a lot of hassle just to get deafened, choked and blinded. You could fall in a cement mixer and have all the same stuff going for you.'

Ned laughed. 'I like it.' He looked at Tabby through his mirror. 'Your friend's a real wit, Tab.'

Tabby nodded. 'I know. That's why she's along.'

'Anyway.' The reflected eyes switched to me. 'You're about to find out for yourself, Zoe. We're here.'

Ned steered the car into the curb and stopped. I looked out and saw what looked like a poky old shop in a dilapidated row. Its window was boarded up and somebody had daubed 'Blue Moon' across the boards with blue paint. The paint had run down in lines so that the words seemed propped on spindly legs. Beside the window a door stood open and the strip of brickwork between supported a man in dark glasses who was chewing a match.

The man watched us get out of the car. As we approached the door he pushed himself upright and stood with his hands in his pockets, blocking our way.

'Two bucks,' he mumbled. 'Each.'

Ned produced a handful of coins and began counting them into the man's palm. The guy rolled the match from one corner of his mouth to the other and said, 'Been saving up, kid?' Ned was unloading small change on him and I guess he'd have preferred notes. With his shades and thin moustache he looked sort of sinister. I wouldn't have risked answering back, but Ned said, 'It's money isn't it?' and the guy just shrugged.

All the time Ned was counting, people kept going in the door. Larry noticed this and said, 'Hey!' The man's eyes flicked up.

'Whassamarra, kid?'

'Them.' Larry pointed at two guys just walking in.

'What about them?'

'What about 'em?'

'They haven't paid. Why do we have to pay and not them?'

The guy sneered. 'What they gonna pay with kid – foodstamps? Subbies got all the peanuts.'

Chippies hardly ever get cash. Even I know that, for pete's sake. For all that he's the son of a Selectman, Larry can be very dumb sometimes.

When the guy finally let us in we followed Ned along a short passage into a large, crowded room. People sat hunched over little tables with drinks in front of them, and most of the space between was filled with people standing. There was a bar along one wall and an alcove in another, stacked with sound equipment. A DJ was feeding an ancient twindeck. He had the volume so high you felt it through your feet. Near the alcove some people were trying to dance on a raised platform the size of a Kleenex. The atmosphere was ninety percent smoke and there was a nauseating smell whose cause I didn't want to think about.

We were standing in the doorway. Ned turned and said something I didn't catch. I leaned toward him. 'What?'

He shoved his lips in my ear. 'I said, what'll you have?'

I didn't know. I wasn't concentrating. I'd seen a terrific-looking boy across the room. 'What's Tabby having?' I said.

'A lobotomiser.'

'A what?'

'A lobotomiser. It's coke with rum and a couple of other ingredients. Try one?'

'Sure, why not?' I didn't want a drink. I specially didn't want a drink with a name like lobotomiser, but what could I do? I wanted to be part of the gang, and the quickest way to screw up something like that is to act like a drag.

So.

DAZ

Thay com in lucking nervous. 4 of em. 2 guys 2 wumen, nor thay aint old enuff 2 be owt ov school neever. Stop by the door lucking rownd like somfing smell bad. i'm wiv Mick and som ovver guys and we just turn away like we saying you noffing 2 us you Subby trash, only thers 1 of em rite, this girl, and she's nice. Not just 2 luck at. i dont mean that. She coms in diffrent. Lucks rownd diffrent. Not sniffy if you know wot i mean. i cop a luck then turn away wiv the overs and then a bit later i luck rownd and catch er watching me. Soon as i turn er eyes go down but its 2 late i seen er. i gorra be careful cos i don't want Mick 2 see me lucking and him getting ready 2 introdoos me 2 Cal, but i keep watching owt ov my eye corner and she's fixt on me alrite.

ZOE

Ned began making his way towards the bar and the rest of us followed. The Chippies let us through, but they weren't acting pleased to see us and I avoided looking in their eyes.

When we all had drinks, Ned used his height to look for space. He spotted some and we went and stood there, holding our drinks and surveying the scene.

It was no big deal, I can tell you that. Just a lot of mean, dirty people crammed into a tacky room getting smashed, while some psycho of a DJ took out their eardrums to get at their brains. I was already wishing I hadn't come, and I knew if we got home in one piece I was never going to do it again.

It must have shown on my face too, because Tabby nudged me and grinned and pointed to my glass. 'Try it!' she yelled. 'It'll put you in the mood.'

'Or in the hospital,' cried Larry, who looked drunk already.

I sniffed my glass, and it didn't smell like coke. I didn't want to drink it, but I saw the evening in front of me and I sure didn't want to spend all of it feeling the way I was feeling now. I shrugged, lifted the glass to my lips and took a sip.

It wasn't bad. It tasted better than it smelled, and I could feel it making its way down inside me like a hot little elevator. It felt sort of good, if you want to know. I took another sip and that felt even better. It was then

I noticed the glass was dirty, but what a lobotomiser'll do is, it'll relax you, right? Two sips and I was laid back to where I could think, what the heck d'you expect in a dive like this – Waterford Crystal?

In fact it wasn't a bad old place once you got a drink inside you. It was sort of cheerful, really – all these people, laughing and smoking and moving to the music as if they weren't dirty or poor or anything. It was like they left all that outside. They were okay, and we were okay too. What you had to do was, you had to let go and let it sort of sweep you along. I was being swept along, all right. By the time I finished my drink all I knew was I never felt anything like this down the Silverdale youth centre. All of my nervousness had gone and I was ten feet tall.

I must have been on to my third lobotomiser when the boy I'd noticed before turned and looked at me. He was just another Chippy guy in a beat up leather jacket and wild, greasy-looking hair, but he turned round and our eyes met and that was it.

I guess sometimes there are moments when people's lives change and they don't even know it. They can look back later, when everything's different, and say yes, that was the start of it – that's when it all began, and I didn't even notice.

Well, I noticed all right, and it was like – I can't explain. It was like everything shattering apart, y'know? I mean everything. Things I thought I knew. Stuff I'd been taught. The foundation of my life is what I'm talking about here, and I felt it shift, and if you've never felt that then you don't know what I'm talking about. Anyway, it shifted that night and shattered apart and Ma and Pa Askew never got their sweet little Zoe back. Oh, they thought they still had her, but they didn't. It was somebody else.

Somebody else entirely.

DAZ

'Here's Cal now.'

i lucked, and i seen this littel guy wiv spex. Fin he was. Five foot frag-all wiv blond hair and neat doodies like a Subby. i sez, you jest, and Mick sez no, that's im.

i cant beleev it. Like, Cal's a nero, you know? A living ledge end. Peeple tork abowt im all the time. Thers a price on is hed for faxake, and hear he com lucking like a shagged-owt det-clecter.

Aniway he com over and sez somfing 2 Mick and Mick sort of nods at me and nex fing Cal's standing nex 2 me and he sez i'm off 4 a slash, foller in a minit. He gos of tord the bog and Mick does a fumsup wiv a silly grin on is face. i wait and wile i'm waiting i shoot anovver glance tord this Subby girl. She's in a corner wiv er mates. She's lucking at me but drops er eyes wen i luck at er. She's making me feal funny and I wish she never com in tonite. Any ovver nite yes but not tonite. Why'd she hafta com in tonite of all nites, screwing me up, like i'm wondering if all Subbys're bad. Cors all Subbys're bad. Evry 1 knows that.

i go in the bog. Thers 2 guys in, Cal and anovver. i pertend 2 slash and Cal's wiping his hands til the geezer gos. Then he sez strait owt, who's the girl?

My hart kicks. Wot girl i sez, and he sez i seen you lucking at that Subby tart. Guy fancys Subby tarts no good in Dred. How you feel, sposin you gotta kill er? He torks fast, all the time watching the door. Jumpy i guess. i'd be jumpy an all, 50 thou on my hed.

i dont know wot 2 say. Panicking inside finking, i'm blowing it. All that time waiting 2 com 15 and now i get my chance i'm blowing it. i kill er, i sez, no danger, but i'm not so shor and i fink he knows it, but before he can say anyfing else thers this crash like some 1 frou somfing and Cal sort ov freezes, lucking at the door. Then he spins rownd and befor i can breeve he's up and away owt the window.

I never seen any 1 move so fast.

ZOE

We nearly didn't make it. I mean, everything could have ended for the four of us right there in the Blue Moon that night, and it'd all have been Larry's fault.

What happened was, he saw this girl. Chippy girl. She was with another girl and two guys and they might have been married for all we knew but it made no difference to old Larry. She was pretty and he was smashed and he caught her eye and smiled and started making signs for her to leave the others and come on over. I felt quite apprehensive about it in spite of the drink, and so did Ned. He said something to Larry – tried to get him to stop, but Larry accused him of being jealous and went right on doing it. The girl kept smiling, but it was the sort of smile people put on when they're embarrassed and don't know what else to do. I could see that, and I bet Tabby and Ned could too, but not Larry. Oh no. He thought she fancied him and redoubled his efforts.

At first the two guys ignored him. Chippies don't like people from the suburbs and they'd as soon smash a Subby to pulp as not. But there's always big trouble with the police when something like that happens, so unless theyr'e members of Dred or very drunk they'll usually bend over backwards not to get involved. In the face of their seeming indifference, Larry's antics became increasingly gross, until finally he yelled at the top of his voice, 'Come on over honey – you know you're wasted on that trash!' It was just our luck that this outburst coincided with a break in the music. There was this awful silence while everybody in the room turned to look at us, and then one of the two guys – the one who was with this girl I guess – got up and grabbed his chair and came at Larry like he meant to splatter his brain. He probably would've done it too, if two beefy guys hadn't burst on the scene and put themselves between him and us. They must've been lurking somewhere discreetly, watching the trouble build. When the guy saw he wasn't going to reach Larry he let out a roar and flung the chair. Larry threw up his arms to fend it off, and it bounced off him on to the floor. Meanwhile, the two heavies had grabbed the other guy and were wrestling him towards the door.

Larry was hunched over, moaning and holding his arm. There was still no music, and everybody seemed to be watching us. The atmosphere of resentment was unmistakable: there was a sort of murmur, and I had the distinct feeling that the crowd was closing in on us. I was fuddled with the drink, I guess, but I remember thinking, this is it. We'll never make the door. We're gonna die. Tomorrow they'll find the car, and maybe a shoe.

Then I saw him – the guy I'd been looking at all night. I never saw him arrive, but suddenly there he was and he said, 'You better leave with me. Now.' He didn't pause but sort of walked through us, slipping his arm through Larry's on the way past, helping him along.

We didn't hang around.

DAZ

So this crash com and Cal's away. i open the door a crack and luck owt and its wot i fought. Subbys. i knew ther be trubble tonite wiv them in. Stanstareeson dunnit.

i luck and i fink, sod em. They blew it 4 me. Let em get topped. Then i seen the girl. The 1 i bin watching. She luck scairt. 2 hunnerd peeple want me ded, i luck scairt. i seen her and i cant let em do it. The uvvers i dont give a monkeys abowt but i cant let em top her.

Its a tuff 1 cos the peeples real mad and i gotta be cool. i go over nice and easy. i tork soft. i tell em you better leave wiv me now, nor i dont stop neever. i grab this fin Subby wots hurting and shov frou going hello Pete, hows fings Miz Stanton, givin em the big smile. And all the time i'm finking, we not gonna make it. Somfing gonna snap but noffing does and it seems a longtime and then were at the door.

i let go the fin Subby. Run, i sez. i know thay gorra motor near. Thay run. 3 of em. Not her. Run, i sez 2 her. Peeples coming, i sez. Lucking 2 her, 2 them, 2 her. Fanks, she sez, and she kiss my cheek quick and runs. i want 2 say somfing back but i dont know wot. Peeple shoving me. I showt somfing. You nice. i like you. somfing like that, but i dont fink she hears me. A motor starts. Dazzlers com on, moving. Shes away.

After, i cant beleeve i don it. Wot am i, a Subby or somfing? i got bags ov time 2 fink about it anall, cos i

27

sure cant go back in the Blew Moon now. Peeple stairing and muttering.

Mick. He give me this luck like i kick him in the teef and then he turns and gos back in. Evry 1 else gos in 2. i'm on my tod. i luck arownd 4 Cal but no chance. Black streets. A dog far of. Some rain. Home then. Watch the box wiv our mam.

i'm not in Dred, our mam.

That's nice, Daz.

i seen this Subby girl, our mam.

Forget her, Daz.

Not easy, our mam. Not easy.

ZOE

It must've been the shortest Chippy trip ever. Ned kept his foot down all the way and we were back in Silverdale for nine-thirty. Nobody spoke to me till Tabby said g'night when they dropped me off, and it took her all her time to say that. I guess I shouldn't have hung around when it was time to go but the guy had stuck his neck out for us, hadn't he? I couldn't just run off without saying anything.

Anyway, their being mad at me was the least of my worries right then. The worst thing was not being able to get the guy out of my mind. I kept seeing him in that doorway, holding everybody back while we got away. I tried telling myself he was just a Chippy and Chippies aren't like us and all that sort of stuff, but it was no use. I knew he was a hero, even if he was a Chippy. He took our part and he'd suffer for it one way or another.

And it wasn't only that. If it had been I could have handled it, but there was something else. It was like he'd gotten inside my head and I couldn't get him out. His smile. I only saw it once across that crummy room, but it must've printed itself on my eyelids or something because every time I closed them there he was, smiling. I even saw him when my eyes were open. In fact if you want the truth I wasn't seeing or thinking of anything else.

When I got in, Dad said 'How was Alice?'

I had just enough sense left to realise my parents

29

might smell the booze on me and I was heading straight for my room. 'Fine,' I said. 'Sends her love.' Mum gave me this puzzled look as I breezed by but I didn't stop.

I made plenty of noise taking off my shoes and brushing my teeth so they'd think I was going to bed, but I didn't. Not for ages. By a fantastic coincidence which you won't believe, my window faces south, and what I did was, I stood for about three hours looking out. You can't even see the city from my window but I stood there anyway, gazing south and thinking about him.

You don't have to tell me. Crazy, right? I didn't even know his name, but by the time I got into bed one thing had become very clear.

I had to see him again.

You have to understand that is was virtually impossible for a surburbanite to fraternise with a Chippy. People lived, worked and played inside their own suburb or moved at speed between suburbs, and from newtown to newtown. The only Chippies we saw were those who had passes to come into a suburb to work. They came in the mornings and left at dusk, and they did all the crummiest jobs – digging holes in the road, collecting trash, cleaning washrooms. A few were servants or gardeners in big houses, but they had to leave in the afternoon like the rest. You let a Chippy stay the night, he'll rip off all your stuff and maybe cut your throat for an encore. Chippies're envious, see. Full of hate. Even the lucky ones with jobs in the suburbs. Nobody'd even talk to a Chippy except to tell him what to do, and as kids we'd cross the street whenever we'd see one coming.

So that was the fix I was in. I couldn't get this guy out of my mind and I had to see him again, but as far as I knew he didn't have a pass, and I certainly couldn't hope to get invited on another chippying expedition for some time. And even if I did, who's to say they'd choose the Blue Moon? And if they did, why should he be there? He might use a different club every night, for all I knew.

I moped. I couldn't eat. Couldn't concentrate. I started avoiding company, and of course Mum noticed the change in me and mentioned it and I damn near bit her head off.

Finally I did what I always did when things got rough for me. I went and talked to Grandma.

She's one hundred and four years old and she's still got all her marbles. That's not all that unusual in the suburbs, of course. If she'd been a Chippy she'd have been dead fifty years. She's Mum's grandma, not mine, and she sees things differently. I mean, everybody else I know feels more or less the same about most things. I could tell my parents about some problem I was having, or I could talk to one of the teachers at school or I could go to a preacher, and they'd all say the same things, and I'd know all the things they were going to say before they said them. Like, suppose I told about this Chippy guy, right? How I happened to meet him and how I

31

couldn't sleep and all that. Well, it wouldn't matter who I was talking to, they'd start by saying I shouldn't have been chippying in the first place, and then they'd tell me Chippies're not like us – they don't have the same feelings, so it's a mistake to get emotionally involved with one. They'd say that of course any further contact between this guy and me was out of the question, and finish by telling me I wasn't really in love anyway – I was too young. Somewhere along the way they'd probably ask me whose idea it was to go chippying, so my original problem would still be there and I'd have a new one because I refused to give them a name.

So I went to see Grandma. She has an apartment in a senior citizens' block in another part of Silverdale. Wentworth Apartments. I hope I don't need to tell you who put it up. This was a Saturday, by the way, two weeks after the fateful trip. I flashed my ID for the guy on the door, rode the elevator up and rang the bell. I had to wait a bit. Grandma has a quick mind but her legs're slowing down some. She smiled when she opened the door.

'Zoe. How nice.' She peered at me. 'Is something the matter, dear?'

I shrugged and smiled. 'Nothing much, Grandma. I've got to talk to someone, that's all.'

'Then you've picked the right someone.' She's terrific, old Grandma. I mean, if I was a hundred and four I'm sure I'd be too busy wondering how much time I had left and what happens after you die to want to be bothered with other people's problems. Grandma's not like that. She takes the time to listen. Time's the one thing I have, she'll say.

She put me in a chair and fixed coffee like she was the kid and I was the old lady. When it was done she sat down facing me and said, 'Now – what's troubling young Zoe, eh?'

I told her. When I was through she sat for a long time, gazing into her coffee cup. I sipped from mine, thinking, she's stumped. First time ever. She doesn't know what to say to me.

Then she started talking, very softly. She didn't look up at me. It was like she was talking to herself. 'I was sixteen,' she said, 'and working in a music shop in Rawhampton city centre. One day a boy came in. A young man, really. Eighteen or nineteen.' She smiled. 'The instant I saw him my heart kicked me so hard in the ribs I couldn't get my breath. I thought I'd die, right there behind the counter. He didn't come to me. I was on records and he wanted a cassette. This friend of mine, Pauline, was on the cassette counter and he went to her. I stood and stared all the time she was attending to him. He was the most gorgeous creature I'd ever seen and I couldn't tear my eyes away. If the boss had come in just then I'd probably have got the sack, but I couldn't help it.' She smiled, lifted her cup and sipped. 'I followed him with my eyes as he left the shop. We didn't have the cassette he wanted and Pauline was ordering it for him. I went across to look at his name on the order pad. I've never forgotten it. It was Gordon Payne, and it rang bells for me. I couldn't understand why Pauline hadn't passed out with excitement, but when I asked her when he was calling in again she said "Tuesday" in a matter-of-fact voice and slid the pad back under the counter.

'Tuesday.' Grandma sighed. 'Of course, I can't remember now whether it was a Tuesday or some other day. It doesn't matter. The point is, it was four or five days before I saw him again, and during that time I was in torment. I couldn't eat. I couldn't sleep. I mooned all day and neglected my work. I lost interest in my friends and the things I liked to do. I somehow managed to convince myself that he'd noticed me, that he was pining

33

for me right now as I was for him, and that when Tuesday came he'd declare his love and we'd live happily ever after.'

She paused and looked at me. 'He didn't, of course. I'd waited all that morning in what the novelists call an agony of suspense, and when he came in he collected his cassette, paid and left. He hadn't even glanced in my direction and I never saw him again, but it was months before I stopped hoping. Months.'

She sipped her coffee and I said, 'You're warning me, right? You're saying he's probably forgotten me already.'

'I'm saying it's a possibility you should bear in mind, Zoe. It could save you some pain, though of course it'll cause you some, too.' She smiled. 'There was a song – oh, before my time even. "Love Hurts" it was called, and that's what I'm trying to say. It hurts, even when it's got everything going for it. When it hasn't it hurts more, and this love of yours has nothing going for it. Nothing at all.'

She meant, with him being a Chippy and all, but she didn't call it impossible or tell me I only thought I was in love, and that's what I mean about Grandma.

I nodded. 'I know.' My voice was shaky with trying not to cry. 'But I've got to see him again, Grandma. I've just got to.'

I cried then. I couldn't help it. I slid down off my chair and knelt on the carpet and buried my face in her lap like I used to when I was very small, and she stroked my hair. Neither of us spoke for a while, and then Grandma said, still stroking my hair, 'Wait, Zoe. It's all you can do. If this boy feels anything for you he'll find a way to tell you so. And if he doesn't, you'll be left riding out the pain, as I was.'

It sounded a bleak prospect. I mean, maybe the guy wasn't feeling anything for me right now – he only saw me once, for a few hectic seconds. If we could meet again in different circumstances –.

I sniffled and said, 'Couldn't I go there, Grandma? Back to the Blue Moon?' I felt her shake her head.

'Better not, Zoe. Wait. I know it's hard. It's one of the hardest things there is, but you know we can't make people love us. It happens, or it doesn't. I hope it happens for you, but if it does it'll only be the start of your real worries.' She ruffled my hair and stirred and I lifted my face, leaving a damp place on her skirt. I said, 'I feel much better, Grandma, now I've talked to you.' It was true.

'I feel better too,' she said. 'Perhaps I'm getting over Gordon Payne.'

DAZ

Mister James sez Wots got in 2 you Darren? He calls me Darren. its a fursday and i'm in school. i dint jack it in cos i'm not in Dred. Well its som wear to go innit.

Noffing sir i sez, but thats a fib. somfing got in 2 me alrite and i know wot. Subby girl got in 2 me but i cant tell him that, can i?

It screwed evryfing up, that nite. Evryfing. i wish it never happen but it did. i cant stop finking abowt her, even thogh i know she dont give a monkeys abowt me. Subbys dont fink we human even, but i fink abowt her all the time. How she hung abowt 2 say fanks. Kiss me. Gotta mean somfing, rite?

Rong. Dont mean noffing. Subby trash playing arownd, like thay do. i wish i never helpt em. i do. Mick stopt coming 2 school. He's in Dred. Only com 2 school cos i do and now hes gon. Week after that nite i call rownd his place. Arst him 2 fix anovver meeting wiv Cal. Yor joking, he sez. Cal risk his life 4 you and wot dos he see – he sees a guying lucking at Subbys like he lovs em. Sees a guy sooner help Subbys than his own sort. Own famly, mebbe. You make a prat outa me Daz, he sez, and nobody makes a prat outa me. Bog off he sez, and dont you com rownd no more.

i want 2 join Dred. i do, but i keep seeing Cal. Jumpy Cal. The luck in his eyes. The way he went frou that window.

So evryfings mucked up, rite? Only 1 happy our mam

and she dont know abowt the girl. If she did she wont
be 2 happy neever i can tell you.

Aniway thats wots got in 2 Darren Mister James.
Noffing.

ZOE

I really did feel better after I talked to Grandma. I'd been hatching all sorts of wild plans aimed at getting back to the Blue Moon, torturing myself with pictures of him finding someone, telling myself I could be that someone if only I wasn't trapped in a cage called Silverdale. Now I found I had the strength to shut out these thoughts, and it was one less thing to fret about. It's out of my hands, I told myself. I can only wait. It was sort of restful for a while.

I'm not saying it was easy. It wasn't. Waiting for something you really, really want and probably won't get is terrible, and it's particularly bad if you can't share it with those around you. I mean I couldn't say to my parents, oh by the way if you find me a little tense these days don't worry. I'm expecting a message from this Chippy guy I met, or maybe even a midnight visit, and if it happens we just might go off together. I couldn't tell them I was under a strain, and so I had to try to be my old sweet self, answering politely when they asked about school and friends and things like that – stuff I didn't care about anymore. It affected me in various unexpected ways.

Like that same Saturday. That day, while I was visiting with Grandma there'd been some sort of disturbance in the city. A riot. It happens a lot, and there's usually a bit on the news about it, and then Dad will have something to say about Chippies and what he'd

38

do to them if he were the government. He always says
the same things, and I don't pay it any heed because
it's just an automatic response with him and it's not
important, anyway – he's never going to be the government. Mum doesn't pay it any heed either – maybe she
doesn't even hear it anymore. Anyway, this item comes
on screen and Dad says 'Riot? I'd give 'em riot. I'd
have a door-gunner in every 'copter and cream 'em.'
He snorts. 'They'd think twice before they'd riot again,
I can tell you.'

As I say, he'd said it all before, only this time I got a
picture of Chippies crumpling under a hail of lead, and
one of them was you know who. I said, 'They're people,
Dad. Some of them're probably nice if you know them.'

He looked at me sharply, then his startled expression
softened into a sneer. 'Nice? I'll tell you how nice they
are, Zoe. One night a couple of months ago a bunch of
Fairlawn kids drove into the city. Their folks thought
they were visiting Goldengrove, and when they hadn't
returned at midnight a parent raised the alarm.' He
paused to create some suspense. 'They found them next
day, four of 'em, hanging by their feet on the forecourt
of a derelict gas station, shot through the back of the
neck.'

Mum said 'Gerald!' – like that. I guess she thought
Dad ought not to have told me this horrible story but
it was all right. I'd heard it ages ago from Tabby, who
likes such things. I said 'That was Dred, Dad. They're
not all in Dred. Most of them're just poor folks getting
along the best way they can.'

'Oh yeah?' I could see he was getting mad but I was
mad too. 'And just what in the bright blue blazes d'you
think you know about it, Zoe? You, who've never so
much as set foot outside of Silverdale in the whole of
your spoiled little life?'

I wanted to tell him then. Oh, I did. About the trash

and the dogs and the Blue Moon and Chippy eyes up close. The crowd closing in and the way we were saved. I wanted to see the look on his face but of course I couldn't so I said, 'Grandma says they're people like you and me.'

'Grandma's an old lady,' he said. 'Her savvy's out to lunch.'

Mum shot him a look because this was vulgar and also untrue. I didn't say anything. I got up and walked out and went to my room and drew a helicopter and wrote 'FAN' underneath in big letters and left it around for him to find. Fan's a Chippy word and he hates me using Chippy words.

○ □ ○

So I was in trouble at home. This was on top of my original problem, plus the fact that my few friends were cooling off from neglect and I couldn't get interested in anything.

Then, just as it began to seem that nothing would ever be right again, something else went wrong.

I got in trouble at school, and this was something new for me. I believe in keeping my head down so I don't get noticed, and this has usually worked. I never got detentions or counselling or any of that stuff. Not until this day I'm going to tell about.

It was a Monday – the Monday after my Saturday clash with Dad. Modern History with Miss Moncrieff. I've never liked old Moncrieff and I usually switch off in her class because history's so boring. Dates, dust and deadmen, right?

Anyway, it was Modern History and I was looking out of the window. It was one of those gorgeous mornings you sometimes get in October when the sun shines through mist and makes it look like gold, and the dew's still on the grass and that's gold too, and all the trees are red and gold and there are spider webs made of crystal lace. I was looking out the window, wishing I was out there walking hand in hand with you know who, and Moncrieff's voice was droning on in the background. She was talking about something called the Franchise (Income Qualification) Bill of 2004. (Yawn, yawn.) Not the most riveting stuff, even the first time around, and this was the second time around because we were revising for the November exams. Well – the others were. I was rehearsing something else entirely.

Anyway she's on about this bill and she must've spotted that I wasn't paying attention and she stops droning and goes, 'Why did the Dennison government introduce this bill, Zoe Askew?'

'What bill, Miss?' I asked. Well, she took me by surprise.

'The bill I've been talking about for the last half hour while you've been gazing out the window.'

'I don't know, Miss.'

You could tell she didn't like it. She grew very still. Her cheeks went white and twitched a couple of times as she looked at me. I felt quite nervous. I thought she might flip and fling herself at me, screaming.

She didn't. Instead she started speaking, softly and very distinctly, moving her mouth in an exaggerated way like I was just learning to lip-read or something. 'The Franchise (Income Qualification) Bill was introduced to correct an anomaly whereby those sections of the population which contributed least to society were able to exercise undue influence upon it through misuse of the vote.' She looked at me. 'Do you think you can remember that?'

'Yes, Miss.'

'Good.' She smiled like a shark. 'Because when you go home this afternoon you will write it out forty-five times, word for word in your neatest hand – that's one time for each minute you've wasted in my class today.'

Some of the kids tittered and she froze them with her gorgon special. That's a look she gives which damn near turns you to stone. She thought they were laughing at me but they weren't. I knew why they were laughing. They were thinking, we've all wasted the forty-five minutes, Miss – that's what your classes are – a waste of time, but of course nobody would say it. I was the only one dumb enough to talk back to old Moncrieff.

I know what you're thinking. You're thinking, is that it? Is that what you call trouble – a few stupid lines to write out?

Well, no it isn't. We haven't got to the trouble yet. That's coming up next, as they say on telly.

DAZ

Dred gud, Subbys bad
Dred gud, Subbys bad
Dred gud, Subbys bad
Dred gud, Subbys bad
Dred gud, Subbys bad
Dred gud, Subbys bad
Dred gud, Subbys bad

i rite this all down my maffs book.

   Mister James sez, you spose to be doing maffs.

   Wot's a maff, i sez, so he frow me owt, nor I can't go
back no more.

   Subbys call it Chippy grad you ayshon.

ZOE

I did it. I wrote it out forty-five times in my neatest hand and it took all evening. It was a drag all right, but when Moncrieff tells you to do something it's best to do it.

I did it, and then I sat looking at it for a long time in the light from my desktop lamp. I'd filled thirteen sheets of paper. Thirteen, and I knew exactly what she'd do when I handed them to her because I'd seen her do it to other kids. She wouldn't read them. She'd riffle through to make sure I hadn't slipped in any blanks. If all the sheets were filled and the whole thing looked neat she'd tear it in half and dump it in her wastepaper basket. Three hours to produce, three seconds to dispose of. Part of the punishment, right? If she found sloppy work or blanks she'd have me do the whole thing again.

Anyway, I sat looking at it, and then I pulled the last sheet towards me and scrawled 'Brainwashing' across the bottom. I don't know if you're familiar with that term. Brainwashing. I am, because Grandma uses it all the time. She says half of what's on TV and in the papers is brainwashing, and she reckons a lot of what they teach us in school is brainwashing too. When I asked her what brainwashing is, she told me it's repeating lies over and over till people come to believe them. She says Dad's the most brainwashed person she ever met. I looked at what Moncrieff had made me write and I thought, this is brainwashing. What the Dennison government did was take the vote away from the Chippies, and what I've just written out forty-five times is the excuse they gave for doing it. Repeating lies over and over till –.

Well, it hadn't worked with Grandma, and it wasn't going to work with me, and that's why I wrote 'Brainwashing' across the last sheet. I'd like to claim I did it for old Moncrieff, but I didn't. Like I said, she never reads kids' lines, so I knew she'd never see it. It was a gesture, I guess. Just a gesture. Trouble is, Moncrieff chose that Tuesday morning to break the habit of a lifetime.

DAZ

Wen you fink abowt some 1 all the time and you cant see them its bad. Wen you got noffing els 2 do its worse. I got noffing els 2 do now.

1 day i'm sitting in the flat finking as usual and i remember somfing this guy Clint shown me longtime back. Clint you basted you ded 2 years now and serve you rite. This Clint hes in Dred wiv our Del rite? Hes in Dred but i dont know why thay want him. Hes got a big mouf, Clint. Aster let peeple know wot hes doing all the time. Aster be a nero.

Aniway its him wot gets our Del topped. Him and his big mouf. They done a job togevver see, only the nite before, this Clint he gets drunk and blabs and some 1 over ears him – lornorder mebbe, or a Subby. No 1 knows, but thay waiting and thay get our Del and Clint gets away, nor Del dont split on him neever. But after thay top him this Clint vanishes and no 1 ever sees him again. Evry 1 knows Dred fixt him but no 1 torking abowt it. Any 1 tork Dred biznis gotta be crazy, rite?

Aniway this 1 time – i'm 11 i fink, Clint shown me how Dred get into Silverdale. That's the sort of guy he was – hed show somfing like that to a littel kid. We're way up in the norf part of the city seeing wot we can find, and he luck norf and smile and sez, Silverdale that way. i can go in ther anitime.

o no you cant i sez. i know he got no seeit. No veeza. you cant get in Silverdale any more'n i can, i sez.

46

o yes i can, he sez. Dred way, see?

Wots that, i sez. Dred way?

He shown me. Thers like this big lid rite? In the road. Big iron lid, and Clint he lift it up and thers a hoal wiv a ladder going down and he sez, see that? Thers a tunnel down there wot goes rite inter Silverdale. i dont beleeve him. if it goes inter Silverdale i sez, how come evry 1 dont go? How come guys cut the fence and the dazlers catch em and they get shot?

he larfs. its not just 1 tunnel he sez. its lots of tunnels. You gotta know the way see, or you mite get lost. Wander in the dark til you die. Aniway he sez, any 1 else go in there, Dred top em.

i remember this wot Clint shown me all those years back and i fink well im going frou, Dred or no Dred. When you gotta see some 1, you gotta see em.

i start 2 make a plan.

ZOE

Tuesday morning, breaktime. I take my thirteen sheets along to the staffroom and knock. Moncrieff answers the door herself. She has this bright, enquiring look on her mug but when she sees who it is her features sort of shift around till she's looking at me like I'm a dog turd.

'Yes?'

'Lines, Miss.' I hold out the wad.

'Hmm.' She takes them. I stand looking bored while she riffles through. I'm not going to flinch when she rips them up. I won't even blink. I'll keep this blank expression so she'll know I don't give a toss.

'What's this?'

I focus my eyes. 'Huh?'

'This.' She's waving the thirteenth sheet in my face. 'Brainwashing. What d'you mean by it, eh?'

My heart gives a painful lurch and I swallow hard. For the first time in living memory she actually looks at a set of lines and it has to be mine. Act cool, Zoe kid – it's your only chance. I frown at the paper like I'm seeing it for the first time and I say, 'I dunno, Miss. I guess that must've been there before I wrote the lines.'

She sneers. 'Do you expect me to believe that, Askew?' Askew. It's been Zoe ever since I've been at this school and now it's Askew. This gets me mad. Don't ask me why because I don't know. Like I said before, I'm not the sort of kid who gets in trouble at school. I don't get mad at teachers, I get scared. I guess it must be all this

48

other stuff that's been building up without my realising it. Anyway, whatever it is I'm blazing mad and I hear myself say, 'I don't give a monkey's what you think, Moncrieff.'

It wasn't me. That's all I can say. It just wasn't me. I won't go into all the stuff that went down after I said what I said, but it ended with Moncrieff writing a note to my parents and me taking it home. I say ended, but of course it didn't end there.

DAZ

i make this plan rite, and strait off i hit a snag. 2 snags.

    1. wot if she dont live in Silverdale.
    2. even if she does i dunno witch part.

    well i can get in Silverdale. i cant get in aniwear else. So. i go inter Silverdale and luck 4 her dont i? if she dont live ther 2 bad.

    witch part thogh? i dunno. fousands ov howses in Silverdale. cud be any ov them. and if i find it, wot do i do eh – nock on the door? O yeah i can just seeit. Hello mister Subby i come for your littel girl.

    O rite i'll get her 4 you. wot you do wiv her by the way?

    O we run of togevver. liv in the city. you never see her again.

    O well thats alrite then.

    O.K. so i dont go 2 her howse. Shes yung rite? still at school. fousands ov howses. Not fowsands ov schools. So. i luck 4 schools not schools 4 tiny littel Subbys neever. schools 4 big kids. cant be many ov them in Silverdale. 2, if that many. maybe just 1. So i'm not just a pretty face am i?

    our mam says that.

    nex fing – time. see – i fink ov evryfing. No use getting ther and all the kids inside. so 2 chances

    1. get ther first – watch kids go in.

2. end ov day – watch them leev. thats better cos not 2 long til dark.

i'm riting this plan down. Mister James be prowd ov me.

so here it is. i go frou the tunnel get in Silverdale near sundown. Pertend i got graft there. Find big kids school. hang abowt. if i see her grate. if not tuff.

only 1 more fing – wen? Tonite? no. not enuff time. Gotta take it easy see. fink wot doodies 2 wear. wot 2 take wiv me. stuff like that. You rush inter fings, end up ded. Speshly in tunnels.

ZOE

'What's come over her, Amanda, that's what I'd like to know.'

'God only knows, Gerald. I'm sure I don't.'

This is my parents talking, right? Amanda and Gerald. They're talking about me. I'm there, but they're talking as if I'm not. It's teatime. I've just delivered Moncrieff's note and they've taken turns reading it. I'm the only one who doesn't know what she's put. Dad's in the easy chair and Mum's perched on the arm and I stand on the rug in front of them with my hands behind my back, looking at the floor and shifting my weight from one foot to the other. It's embarrassing.

'First she contradicts me to give us the benefit of her opinion on Chippies, then she mopes and sulks for weeks on end till we're frantic with worry, and now this.' He waves the note at me. 'What's going on Zoe, eh? What's happening to you? D'you want to drive your mother and me crazy or what?'

'May I read the note?' I hold out my hand but he shakes his head and says, 'Never mind the note. You know what prompted Miss Moncrieff to write it so you must have a fair idea what it says. Why did you scrawl "brainwashing" across the lines she gave you?'

'Why did you have to write them in the first place?' This from Mum. 'What were you doing wrong, Zoe?'

I shrugged. 'She gave me lines for looking out the

window.' I considered telling about the misty sunlight and the spider webs and all but it would've been a waste of breath. I said, 'What she made me write is a lie.'

Dad's eyebrows went up. 'Oh, really? What was it exactly?'

I told him and he said 'Who told you it was a lie? Who's been talking to you, Zoe – your grandma?' He's got a thing about Grandma. Thinks she's a bad influence. Once when he was real mad he called her a communist and that caused a fight between Mum and him.

I shook my head. 'Nobody talked to me, Dad. I thought it out. They took the vote away from the Chippies and they knew it was wrong so they made up an excuse and I had to write it out forty-five times and that's brainwashing.'

'Nonsense!' He leaned forward in the chair. 'Now listen here, young woman: I've had it just about up to here with your recent behaviour, and so has your mother. I don't know what triggered it off, but whatever it was it stops – right here, right now.' He stood up, thrusting the note in his pocket. 'Tomorrow morning before your first class, you'll apologise to Miss Moncrieff for having defaced the work she set you, and in the meantime you'll write out those forty-five lines again, for me. And I don't want to find any smart footnotes either. Is that clear?'

It was, and I did it, and it took till nine thirty. I spent from then till about ten-thirty at my window, gazing south. It was raining. Finally I got into bed and lay thinking about how it'd be, apologizing to old Moncrieff.

Maybe I'll kill myself instead.

53

I didn't kill myself or I wouldn't be writing this, would I? Oh, I thought about it. I thought about it for quite a while that night: how I'd leave a note for my parents, forgiving them for their unjust treatment of me. When I failed to appear at breakfast Mum would call, and when I still didn't show up she'd come to my room and there I'd be, pale and cold and very still, but smiling so sweetly that all who beheld me would be struck at once with a sense of my total blamelessness. And then they'd find the note on the bedside unit and read it and boy, would they be sorry. How they'd weep. How they'd wish it could be yesterday again so they could have another chance with me. They'd call me that poor, misunderstood lamb and all like that, but it'd be too late, wouldn't it? I'd be gone, and all the sorrow and repentance in the world wouldn't bring me back.

And that's the snag, right? Because I wouldn't get to see any of this. I wouldn't even know about it. I mean, it'd be fine and dandy if I was going to be sitting somewhere out of sight, looking on. Watching the devastation my simple act had wrought but I wouldn't be, would I? Dead is dead, and there's no satisfaction in revenge if you're not around to enjoy it.

So I stayed alive and apologized to Moncrieff. Oh, how could you, I hear you cry. How did you stand it – the humiliation and all?

Well, I'll tell you in a single word. Galileo.

Let me explain.

Galileo was the guy who invented the telescope, and when he'd invented it he used it to look at the moon and the stars and the planets and all that, and he made a startling discovery. He discovered that the earth didn't stand still like people thought in those days, with the sun and moon and stars going round and round for our especial benefit. No. He saw that it was the earth that moved, round and round the sun. This was a very

54

revolutionary discovery, and Galileo wrote it down so others could share his knowledge.

And that was his big mistake, because the guys in charge back then didn't like his discovery. They wanted everybody to go on believing that the earth was in the middle with everything else going round it. So they sent for Galileo and they said it's not true, what you're saying. It's all lies. And Galileo said no it's not, it's true, and if you don't believe me take a peek through my telescope.

They wouldn't do it, though. They didn't want to know. They said, we want you to say you were mistaken. We want you to tell everybody that. In fact, we command you to. But Galileo shook his head and said, I can't tell 'em that. I'm not mistaken – you are.

And this is where they really got mad. They said, you don't understand. Either you tell everybody you were wrong, or we burn you alive.

Well, now that they'd explained it more clearly Galileo told everybody he'd made a mistake. He said his idea of the universe was wrong, but it was just words, right? He knew all the time he was right, only he said the words they wanted to hear so they wouldn't burn him.

And that's how I apologised to old Moncrieff. I said some words to her so they wouldn't kick me out of school, but I knew all the time me and Grandma were right about brainwashing.

Hang in there, Galileo. Way to go, man!

DAZ

Fursday afternoon i smuggel my stuff owt the flat wile our mam up the helf. She's down wiv the dulleye as usual and gon for her scrip.

i got these coveralls you gotta wear in Veezaville. Blue wiv a big yeller disc so they know yor a Chippy. i got the cap 2. Blue baseball cap. i gotta flashlite and a big ball ov twine.

Cost me all my peanuts but i gotta do it, rite? i wisht i gotta seeit anall but they cost moren i got plus not easy to contact the deela.

i know wot you finking. You finking wots he want wiv twine encha? Well, i tell you. 1 time up the school Mister James tel this story abowt sum guy wayback after go frou this maze. Maze is lots of tunnels like i after go frou. This guy scairt he get lost in this maze, plus its got this monster in it – this miner tour. So wot he does is he has his ball ov twine witch he lets it owt as he goes frou so he can foller it back and if he can i can, see?

Aniway i get all this stuff in a plastic sac and i go norf and luck arownd til i find the lid in the road. 2 many people so i pertend i'm jus passing til thay gon. Then i lift the lid and luck in the hoal. Black hoal. i feel funny lucking down plus it stinks. Troof is, now i'm here i dont feal 2 good abowt going down. i tel myself i dont afta but then i fink ov her and here i go.

its not easy standing on this fin rusty ladder wiv my

sac and i gorra put the lid on fore any 1 coms. i luck down but cant see the bottom. Drop the sac, i sez 2 myself. Take a chance. if it lands in water 2 bad. i drop it and hear a fud so thats okay. i nearly fal off the ladder shifting the lid but i get it on nor i dont fink any 1 seen me neeva but its reely dark and stinky and i'm scairt. i go down the ladder, bits ov it come off on my hands and fall on my hed and 1 bit goes in my mouf and when i spit it makes like a lowd ekco noise and i wisht i never done it.

Longway to the bottom but i make it. Standing in somfing soft and wet. Feel about 4 the sac, finking i hope that flashlite okay. if the drop smasht it i'm not going. No way. i find it and it lites fank god. i shine it about. All bricks wiv wite stuff like wool or spiderweb hanging down. 1 tunnel leading of. Just 1, fank god again. if i seen 2 tunnels i wunt know witch, rite?

its cold. My breff is so lowd i wisht i didn't afta breeve. Water dripping 2 so plenty ov ekco. i keep finking about that miner tour and i dont want to leeve the ladder. Dont tork so daft i sez, only i say it in my hed so no ekco. That Clint go frou, any 1 can. This dont make me feel better cos now i fink abowt Clint goast. No such fing i tel myself but still scairt and not even started yet.

Get a grip i sez inside my hed. Do somfing take yor mind of it ha ha. So i put the flashlite in my teef and get the twine and tie 1 end to the ladder and the flashlite all the time jerking abowt making funny shadders on the bricks only not 2 funny rite? Aniway doing somfing makes me feel better. i tie the sac frou my belt so boaf hands free and i can hold the flashlite in 1 hand and the twine in the ovver. if i stop to fink i be up that ladder like a rat up a shitpipe so i dont. i say help me god and i'm in the tunnel going norf.

i hope.

ZOE

So I didn't get kicked out of school but that doesn't mean everything was okay. Far from it. There's a name they call people who fraternise with Chippies – those who get too pally with the hired help or fix coffee for the guys on the garbage truck or something. Chippy-lover. That's what they call 'em. Now you might think the more love there is around the better, but Chippy-lover's a deadly insult. Folks start calling you that, you're liable to lose friends because the friend of a Chippy-lover is a Chippy-lover, if you see what I mean. And that's what some of the kids called me that day, right after I did my Galileo riff with old Moncrieff. I guess they thought I was sticking up for Chippy rights over the vote thing, and they were right. What they didn't know was why. Not that it'd have made things any better for me if they had. If they'd known little Zoe was totally gone on some flaky guy with long hair and a leather jacket, little Zoe would probably have had to quit school right then and there for her own safety. As it was, it must've looked to them like I'd gone soft on Chippies just to be different or something, and some of them called after me in the yard and then along the street.

I tried to act like it didn't bother me, but it did. I had so few friends I couldn't afford enemies. I hurried off up the street, trying not to look like someone in a hurry and wondering what would happen later when I called for Tabby. Wednesday nights Tabby and me go to youth club, and I pictured myself walking up to her door as usual and ringing the bell, only this time Mrs Wentworth answers it and when she sees it's me she looks down her nose and says, I'm sorry dear, Tabitha won't be joining you this evening, and I can tell from the way she says it that Tabitha won't be joining me any other time either from now on, because she's a Wentworth and Wentworths don't associate with Chippy-lovers.

What I did was, I went a long way round to shake off my tormentors, walking rapidly through drifts of fallen leaves, towards the waste ground just inside the boundary fence where nobody ever goes except cats and little kids, and I never did find out what would have happened at Tabby's place that night, because something happened out there. Something staggering.

DAZ

if you fink i'm wadin frou Subby muck you rong. This tunnel old rite? It was here before Silverdale and no 1 use it no more. Most old tunnels blockt of but sum 1 forgot this 1.

So. No Subby muck. Just rat muck plus rats. i hear em and i seen ther littel eyes. Thay dont bovver me, the rats. Thay reel, like me. Not like that miner tour and Clint goast and moving shadders. Not like the ekco neever. Give me the rats ennitime.

Aniway i'm up this tunnel and evryfing going slow exept my hart, witch its going pretty fast. i'm shining the flashlite on the flor and sides and top, mostly flor, and letting out the twine. Wite stuff hanging down evriwear gets in my hair i dunno wot it is. Miner tour fur, mebbe. its cold like ice down here, but i'm getting use 2 the stink – dont notis it no more. i make so much noise walking and breeving it sownds like thers sum 1 follering but only drippy ekco wen i stop. i'm going on like this, stopping and starting, scairt, but saying easy-peasy, not long now, wen suddenly thers 2 tunnels.

i stop, but my hart speeds up sum more. Dont panic, i sez. Fink. i stand ther wiv these 2 black hoals in front ov me, finking, but it dont do no good. no marks aniwear. no way 2 tel witch way Silverdale. Boaf ways mebbe. Or non. So its a tossup only i got nuffing to toss so i try rite. i remember wot Clint sez abowt gerrin lost

60

down here til i die, and a few steps in i stop 2 check my twine. its okay.

This tunnel difrent thogh. hoals both sides leeding of, and pretty soon it splits again and i after chooz. i fink, if i go rite again i'm gonna sail rite past Silverdale. i go left and i check my twine again. You in a stinky black maze, you check yor twine an all i bet.

Aniway by this time i'm starting 2 wonder does this tunnel reely go 2 Silverdale or was that Clint winding me up. Mebbe this tunnel goes nowear. Mebbe it goes 2 the sea. i seen the sea 1 time. its big. And wile i'm wondering this i see somfing on the flor in frunt ov me. somfing wite and its not hanging down neever. i moov tord it slow, shining the flashlite on it and wen i see wot it is i yell out and my yell ekco and ekco and i neerly turn and run.

its a skelington.

this skelington mouf open like it larfing only noffing much to larf abowt rite? Bits of old doodies on it and legboans stuck in dockmartins. i shine my flashlite over it and then i seen somfing make me glad. i know wot you finking. you finking cant be noffing make me glad near a skelington but you rong. Ded rong. (ha ha geddit?) this skelington on its armboan got this band. plastic armband wiv D on it and this is not D for ded this is D for Dred. this wots left ov 1 Dred and i fink, he been 2 Silverdale i bet. got hit not kilt rite away. tryd 2 get hoam but died here. So. i'm going the rite way rite?

littel voyce in my head sez mebbe not. Mebbe this guy lost like you. Shut yor mouf i sez. Wot you wanta go scair me for eh? i stept over the rags and boans and went on kwick.

i'm scairt alrite but noffing else happened plus no more splits in the tunnel. My ball ov twine getting littel thogh, and just wen i fink mebbe it run owt i see lite ahead.

i head 4 the lite, mooving reel slow, finking, Silverdale owt ther boy. You get cort now, you ded. i creep up 2 the end and luck owt. its been longer than i fought gerrin here. Daylite nearly gon but i see why this tunnel aint blockt of. it coms owt a little hilside. Piles ov muck all rownd. Erf and stoans and smasht up brix and long grass over it like sumplace in the city. i never new they had places like this in Veezaville. 1 pile ov muck rite in frunt ov the tunnel plus fireweed and littel trees. hundreds peeple pass by, no 1 see this hoal.

i go back in, strip off my doodies, get into coveralls and cap. now I'm a Chippy wiv graft in Silverdale. i put my doodies in the sac and hide it in the tunnel. i put the littel ball ov twine on the flor wiv a stoan on top. Then i walk out the hoal and frou the piles ov muck like i done it evry day. Gotta luck cool or sum bouncer ast 4 my seeit and i aint got 1. i'm just finking wear the big kid school wen somfing umbeleevabel happens. i luck rownd and ther she is – the girl i come 4.

troof is stronger than friction, rite?

ZOE

It was like Grandma when Gordon Payne walked in that music shop. My heart kicked and I forgot how to breathe and my legs practically gave way under me. Only thing that went on working was my mind, and that must've gone into overdrive because in the second between me seeing him and him seeing me it processed about fifty thousand thoughts.

First I thought, it's not him. It's some guy who looks like him. It was almost dark, see? Then, when there was no doubt it was him I thought, he's not here because of me. He's got work in Silverdale. When he sees me he'll drop his eyes and walk on by like he never saw me before, 'cause that's what Chippies do.

There were a lot more thoughts I've forgotten. It was my mind trying to shield me, I guess – to protect me from disappointment by refusing to believe or even to hope. If I'd let myself think he was looking for me and it turned out he wasn't I couldn't have stood it. I'd have fallen apart.

Anyway, the second passed and he saw me and I knew the miracle had happened. He was here for me, all right – I could see it in his face. He stopped, and I knew exactly how he was feeling – weak knees, aching chest and a mind racing towards burnout.

It was just like an old, old movie. We stood looking at each other and then we both moved at once, and before we knew it we were clinging together in the

middle of all that squalor and nothing mattered except
to hold on and never, ever, ever let go.

DAZ

Its like she sez. i seen her and dam near got a hartatak. We run togevver and clingon and i forget abowt danger and all that.

So we clingon and i sez wot thay call you. Zoe she sez. i never herd ov it. i tel my name Daz and she larfs. wots funny i sez and she sez Daz thats a washing powda. wel i sez. Zoe sownd like a littel animal or somfing and we boaf larfing.

lots more tork we done that firs nite. Magic it was only no magic in my riting so i stop now. you reed wot Zoe put, you be ther.

ZOE

Yes, that's right – shove it all onto me, Daz. Typical flaming Chippy, as Dad would say.

Ah, but he's right. It was magic. It was. I know it sounds corny and all that, but you really do get so wrapped up in each other you forget everything else. I mean, the guy was risking his life just being there and we didn't even think about it. We were within a few yards of the perimeter fence, a double fence with a floodlit walkway between. All suburbs have them, and every now and then security men patrol the walkway. They operate in pairs, some with dogs. They all carry automatic weapons and a Chippy seen anywhere near a fence after sundown is liable to get shot. There'd be TV cameras dotted about as well, and guys in a post somewhere watching screens. The lights had just come on and there'd be a patrol any minute and there we were, him with this big yellow disc on his overall and a Subby girl in his arms, horsing around and laughing as if it were the most natural thing in the world. It's a wonder either of us lived to tell the tale.

When we finally came up for air, Daz steered me toward a drift of rubble which would hide us from the fence. The floodlights created a pool of deep shadow on our side of the drift so that we'd be practically invisible if anybody came along, which was unlikely. We found a couple of big stones and sat down on them, holding hands.

There was so much to learn. So many things we didn't know about each other. He began telling me how awful it had been, thinking about me day and night, not knowing whether I was thinking of him, and I said it'd been the same for me. He asked how old I was and I told him I was nearly fifteen, though my birthday's in February and that was five months away. He said he'd just gone fifteen.

'D'you go to school?' I asked. I knew Chippies don't have to go, some do, some don't. He told me he got thrown out and when I asked why he grinned and said, 'Fooling around – thinking about you when I should've been thinking about my lessons.'

I nodded. 'I got in trouble for that too, but chucked out – that's a bit rough, surely?'

He shrugged. 'Big city. One school. Plenty kids waiting to go. I was gonna quit anyway.'

'What for? I mean, what d'you do now?'

'Nothing. I wanted to join Dred, only they turned me down.'

'You wanted –.' I looked at him. 'Why'd you want to be in a terrorist organisation, for pete's sake?' I realised I knew pitifully little about him.

'Why?' He looked down, hacking the dirt with the heel of his trainer. 'They topped our Del for a kickoff. And I hate Subbies.'

'I'm a Subby.' Yes, I told myself. And here I am sitting in the dark with the guy. How do I know he's not fixing to cut my throat? I wasn't scared, though. I couldn't believe he'd hurt me. It was unthinkable.

'Yeah.' He loosened a small stone and flicked it away with his toe. 'I know. That's how come they knocked me back.'

'How d'you mean?'

'They saw us. You and me. At the club. They've got me figured for a Subby-lover.'

I nodded. 'My so-called friends've taken to calling me Chippy-lover.'

'Why?' He gripped my hands so tight it hurt. 'Do they know about me?'

'No.' I tried to free my hands. He realised what he was doing and relaxed his grip, but he seemed about to jump up and run.

'No, they don't know about you. How could they? I didn't know about you myself till tonight, did I? And if I had, d'you think I'd have told anyone? I'm not a fool, Daz.'

He chuckled, shaking his head. 'Okay, Zoe. I'm jumpy, right? They find me here, I die. For a minute I thought –.'

'Listen.' I looked in his eyes. 'I think you better go soon, anyway.' He'd laughed, but his reaction had reminded me of the risk he was taking. I told him he'd better go but I didn't want him to, and so to keep him I said, 'Who was Del?'

'My brother. He was fifteen.'

'And they – executed him?'

'Topped him, yeah.'

'What for.'

'Dred. Here in Silverdale two years back. I said I'd get even.'

'And will you?' I didn't want to know the answer to that. I don't know why I asked. He shrugged.

'Dunno. Spect so. Have to wait and see, won't we?'

He got up, so I did too. Muted voices and the clop of boots on cement told us a patrol was passing and we stood quietly till the sound receded.

'Listen,' I murmured. 'You better not come here again, Daz. It's too dangerous, but how am I going to see you?'

He shook his head. 'I dunno, Zoe. There's only the tunnel. I gotta see you.'

'Maybe I could come to you.'

'D'you drive?'

'No. You've got to be seventeen.'

'How, then?'

'I don't know. Listen. Is there some way I can get a message to you?' Mail service is confined to the suburbs and so is the phone, so I wasn't going to be able to write or call.

He thought for a minute, then said, 'Mebbe.'

'How?'

'You know the guys who take your trash?'

'Yes I do, but – hey – you mean they'd take a note or something? Wouldn't they get in trouble?'

He laughed. 'Who's going to find one little bit of paper on a trash truck? You slip 'em a little cash, they take your note. Tell 'em Daz at the Black Diamond. It's a club.'

It was obvious when you thought about it, but to me right then it was a wonderful discovery. A lifeline. A means of communication where I'd thought there could be none. For one thing, it meant we could part tonight without too much anguish. It still wouldn't be perfect but it would be bearable.

And that's it. The story of our first date. I told him I'd think of a plan and write him, and meanwhile he was to look at the moon each night at ten and I'd be looking at it, too.

Romantic, right? And easy, because everything was going to be so much better now. So much better. Except that after he insisted on seeing me safely on to a well-lighted road, and kissed me, and melted away in the shadows, my blissful sleepwalk home was shattered first by a shout somewhere behind, then by that unmistakeable ripping noise an auto rifle makes.

I tried to tell myself it had nothing to do with Daz

69

but I knew better, and so after that one brief, ecstatic interlude it was back to square one, only worse.

DAZ

i kist her and it made me feel so grate i forgot wear i
was. Not 4 long thogh. I'm walking under trees, finking
i'm okay in the dark and all, wen sudenly this dazler
hits me in the face and a voice sez hold it rite ther.

i'm blind but not darft. i hang abowt, this guy eever
gonna shoot me or ast 4 my seeit witch i haven't got 1.
Eever way it com 2 the same fing so i run, nor i dont
know wear i run neever.

He dont mess about. i'm dodging frou the trees and
he showt somfing and start shooting. bullits ratling
twigs. i'm so scairt i cant fink. i run and tork like this –
wear the tunnel o god wears that godam tunnel. i'm
crying if you wanta know. Sum basted shoot at you,
you cry 2.

if this guy coud shoot i'm ded rite now. if he foller
me, same. He cant shoot and he dont foller, but wen
the shooting stopt i know he be calling his mates on
radio. soon be milyons of em lucking 4 me. i run til i
seen the fence then cut left along it, blowing and torking
that tunnel o god wears it gon. Soon i'm in piles of muck
and trash and i fink this is it – that tunnel come owt
somwear hear. jus then i hear a big noyz and its a fan
coming innit. Fans got spotlites plus masheenguns. jus
wot i need i dont fink. Fan coming in low over the fence
and i seen it spotlite racing over the grownd and i fink
this is it lad – you ded now 4 shor, but just then i seen
the tunnel. i'm ded nackerd but i run 2 it and get in

71

nor i dont give a monkeys about no miner tour neever.

Not much more 2 tel. i dont stop 2 swop doodies. i grab the bag and set of, wynding in the twine. Slow job that wynding, speshly if sum 1 after you wiv a gun. i dont yuse the flashlite 4 a bit in case they seeit plus i cant stop 2 get it owt.

Aniway, no 1 after me. big noyz outside – yells, fans, shooting. i dunno wot they shooting. each ovver i hoap. after i bang my hed abowt six milyon times i stop and get my flashlite owt the bag and evryfing fine after that. No miner tour. no Clint goast. Skelington stil ther but so wot – damsite wors if he walking abowt rite?

So i get hoam okay and that wen i start 2 worry. Zoe. she herd shooting mebbe she fink i'm ded nor i cant tel her i'm not. Mebbe they pick her up 4 Chippy-lover 2.

So big worry but worf it thogh. O yes.

Zoe.

ZOE

When I got home Mum wanted to know why there was mud on my shoes. It wasn't the number one topic on my mind. I told her I crossed the school playing-field. She didn't know anything about the name-calling and I wasn't about to tell her.

I couldn't eat. I mumbled some excuse about a big school lunch and cleaned up my shoes while my parents ate. After that I went to my room and tried to do my homework. I couldn't concentrate. A voice in my head kept saying, he could be dead. You were with him an hour ago and now he could be dead.

I'd have to watch the news. There's this bulletin at nine o'clock. Normally I'd have been walking back from youth club with Tabby at that time, but I couldn't go now. I told Mum I wasn't feeling too good and stayed in my room, looking out the window. If there weren't houses between I could've seen the fence from here, close to where the tunnel was. As it was I could only see the faint radiance floodlights make in the sky.

Around seven the phone rang in the downstairs hallway. I hoped it was Tabby. Mum would say I was sick but at least it'd mean she was still allowed to associate with me.

It seemed like years till nine o'clock. At five to I switched on my set and caught the weather forecast. Wind and rain. Who cares?

There was nothing on the news. There wouldn't be

in the main bulletin, of course, but there was nothing in the Silverdale spot, either. No news is good news, right?

Wrong. Not for me, anyway. I knew I was in for a sleepless night with plenty of tenterhooks, before the next bulletin at six a.m.

I was right. If you've ever stayed awake all night – one of those long autumn nights – you'll know how the time can drag. I rolled around till my blankets got all knotted up. I drank water and looked at my watch and went to the bathroom about eight hundred times and grew steadily more convinced that Daz was dead. Just before six I switched on with the volume real low and sat on the edge of my wrecked bed squinting at the screen and there is was, first item in the local news:

> 'There was an incident in south Silverdale last night when remote surveillance showed a man acting suspiciously near the perimeter fence. When challenged by a security guard the man, who was wearing outsider coveralls fled, ignoring repeated orders to halt. The guard opened fire but the man made off into the darkness. An exhaustive search failed to find him, and people living in the area are warned to be vigilant since the man is almost certainly dangerous and may be armed.'

Alive! My eyes burned, I looked like a lunatic in an old horror movie and I was starting a headache but I got up and danced round the room, waving my arms, swooping by the mirror to grin at the frightful image I saw there. I took care not to stomp, because I didn't want to wake my parents. I realised I was probably the only person in Silverdale who was glad the intruder hadn't been shot, and I didn't care. Let them stare. Let them call me names. Let them ostracize me for his sake if it suits their tiny minds.

He's alive.

DAZ

So Zoe knew i was okay but i dint know that. i'm worrid she be worrid so wot i done is, i went up 2 the dump. Dump is wear trash trucks go 2 empty plus the deepo is ther. i fort mebbe i fynd the crew wot graft rownd Zoe way and thay can slip her a noat. i know wot Zoe way called. she told me.

i go up ther and ast arownd a bit and shorenuf i fynd the rite crew. 2 snags. 1 this fursday and thay dont work Zoe way til saterday. 2 crewboss nosy. 'What you,' he sez. 'Subby-lover or somfing?'

'Non ov yor biznis,' i sez.

'Not easy,' he sez, 'tork 2 a Subby kid. Trashman tork 2 Subby kids loos seeit, mebbe, loos job.' Corshous littel basted this crewboss but fond ov peanuts, same evrybody.

'Lissen' i sez. 'This Subby kid rich, rite? mebbe got peanuts 4 you, plus a noat 4 me. she be lucking owt 4 you, see – you chicken or wot?'

He tuck my noat. 'fanks mate,' i sez. 'fanks a lot.' not easy 2 smuggel anifing in 2 Silverdale (or any ovver veezaville i gess) evry crew searcht at the gate. easy 2 smuggel stuff owt cos whos gonna fynd 1 littel fing in a truckful ov trash? aniway he tuck it and i'm finking thats better. Zoe know i'm alrite saterday.

i'm going back frou the dump wen i herd futsteps behynd and sum 1 grab me and its Mick and a guy i dont know. thay frow me down in the muck and this guy neal on my back and twist my arm wile Mick jerk my hed up by the hare. 'Lissen,' he sez. 'This from Cal. Cal knows you went frou the tunnel, got shot at. he finks mebbe the Subbies fynd the tunnel cos ov you.' he slam my face in the muck, jerk it up again. blud in my nose and mouf plus loos teef and eyes water. 'Cal sez stay owt ov that tunnel, understand?' i understand but befor i can tel him he slam me down again, jerk me up. 'Understand?' a gud explainer old Mick but i cant tork, mouf ful ov muck and blud and teef. i nod my hed a littel but he done it again aniway and i fink, hes gonna kill me, but he dont do it nomore. the ovver guy get of my back so i can breev, only not 2 gud breeving blud and snot and bits ov toof. i roll over and sit up, holding my face. Mick kick me in the kidnies, sez 'thay find that tunnel, we be back 2 finish you.'

i sit a longtime holding my face witch it hurt very bad. no 1 com 2 help. You help Cal enemy, you Cal enemy 2 and no 1 needs that. So. i sit a longtime in the muck, then i get up and go hoam and tel our mam i fel off a nellifant.

'You darft our Daz,' she sez, and shes rite. And you know wot make me darft?

luv.

ZOE

Saturday. One of those raw, foggy days when it never seems to get light. I'd written a note the night before and now I was hanging around with the thing in my pocket, waiting for the trash truck. I stood in the window looking down the garden. Naked trees, the lawn and pathway slimy with fallen leaves. I hoped the truck would be early. I go for Tabby around ten on Saturdays and my parents might notice if I broke my routine.

Tabby had been sort of distant with me since my clash with Moncrieff over those stupid lines, though she had come up to me in the schoolyard Thursday morning and said she hoped I was feeling better. I'd forgotten I was supposed to be sick and almost gave myself away. I told her it wasn't anything much and we chatted awhile, but there was a coolness about her which made me feel uncomfortable. It was as if in talking to me she was doing something she'd been advised not to do, and I wouldn't be surprised at that.

It must've been my lucky day because the truck came quite early, and as it drew up Mum called me. I went through to the kitchen and she handed me a bag of trash. 'Be an angel and go put this by the can. It's almost full and they might as well take it.

I could've hugged her. I'd dreamed up an excuse to go down the garden just as the crew arrived, but it wasn't nearly as good as this one. I grinned. 'Sure,

Mum. It'll be a pleasure.' She probably thought I was nuts.

I took my time, and the garden gate opened just as I reached the can. The crewman gave me a little nod, with his eyes down the way they do, but as I put down the sack he moved up real close, hissed, 'Here – take it,' and thrust a crumpled bit of paper in my hand.

I knew what it was and my heart kicked. I shoved it in my pocket, hoping nobody was watching from the house. As the guy went to pick up the sack I drew out my own note and slipped it to him. 'Daz,' I whispered. 'Black Diamond. The money's for you.' I'd folded a couple of bills in the note. He nodded, looking past me at the house. I turned and walked away.

'Did that man speak to you?' asked Mum as I came in. She'd watched through the kitchen window. I nodded, trying to look cool. 'Yeah, y'know – rough weather, cold work. Something like that.'

'Well, I hope you didn't encourage him, dear. They're here to work, not fraternize.'

'I know, Mum. I didn't encourage him.' It must be tough having a Chippy-lover for a kid.

Like I said, it must've been my lucky day. The spelling wasn't hot but what he'd written was beautiful. I read it over till I had it by heart, then shredded the note and flushed it down the john. I hated doing that, but to keep it would've been just too dangerous. And after that I got my coat and set off for the Wentworth residence. My luck might continue – who knows?

○ □ ○

It did continue, but it threw up a bit of a mystery as well. See what you make of it.

I arrived at five to ten and rang the bell. This Chippy girl, Zena, usually answers. She's a sort of maid but she doesn't live in. That's not permitted, and I sometimes used to wonder how she coped with the contrast between the beautiful house she worked in all day and the dump she went back to at night. Anyway, she didn't answer this time. Nobody did at first, and I was just telling myself they weren't going to when an eye appeared at the peephole and the door opened, and it was the guy himself. Paul Wentworth, Tabby's old man. He'd a peculiar look on his face and I thought, this is it – he's going to tell me to get lost, but he didn't. He said, 'Come on in, Zoe,' and as he said it his eyes were darting around like he was trying to see in all directions at once. He shut the door so fast I almost lost a foot.

He took my coat and asked how I was and if Mum and Dad were well, but I could tell he was thinking about something else. He put me in the library (no, I'm not kidding – the Wentworth residence has its own library) and went off to get Tabby.

I was standing on a rug so thick it practically reached my knees, warming myself by the fire and gazing round at all the books when Tabby came in.

'Hi.' She grinned her old grin and I felt really good. 'Hi, Tabby,' I said. 'Where's Zena?'

'Oh, we – she's not here anymore. What shall we do today?'

Quick change of subject. I looked at her. 'Is something wrong, Tabby?'

She shook her head. 'No, 'course not. Why should there be?'

'Your Dad. He seemed – I dunno – sort of nervous. Has something happened?'

'No. Not really. Listen.' She put her hand on my

79

arm. 'If I'm a bit cool at school – if I seem to go along
with the other kids when they tease you, it's because I
have to, Zoe. I can't explain. Not now. But I want you
to know I'm the same friend I always was.' She smiled
and squeezed my arm. 'We all are, in this house. Okay?'

I nodded and smiled and said okay, but I wasn't
satisfied. I felt sure there was something going on that
I wasn't supposed to ask about so I didn't, and we went
up to Tabby's room and played some of her fabulous
records and talked about boys and clothes and all that,
and lunchtime we went down Chiefy's for hamburgers,
but it wasn't like it used to be. I'd intended telling her
all about Daz – the notes and everything, but I didn't.
At three-thirty when I was leaving she squeezed my
arm again and said 'remember' with tears in her eyes,
and I walked home not knowing whether the day had
made things better or worse.

And when I walked in the house the police were
waiting.

'Hello, Zoe. I'm Lieutenant Pohlman, Domestic Security. This is Sergeant Daws. We'd like to talk to you if
that's all right.'

Domestic Security. Sounds cosy, right? Forget it.
Domestic Security's the outfit that spies on Subbies and
shoots Chippies. The outfit responsible for keeping us
in and them out. They're the guys the government pays
to keep everything jogging along exactly the way it is,
and they'll do just about anything to see that it does.

So when the lieutenant said we'd like, and if that's alright, I knew he wasn't offering me choices.

I don't mind admitting I was scared. Everybody's scared of DS, but I wasn't so much scared for myself as for Daz. Oh, I knew this could only be about him, and if DS knew about us then whatever they did to me would be nothing compared with what they'd do to him. I assumed they'd intercepted my note and I wondered briefly what had become of the trash crew.

Dad and Mum tried to talk to me but Pohlman got between us and said something to Daws and the sergeant ushered them out the room like it was his house and they were the callers. I heard Mum say she's fourteen for godsake, and then the door closed and it was just me and the lieutenant.

He told me to sit down which was just as well, because I'd probably have fallen down if he hadn't. He took the other chair and said 'Where you been today, Zoe?' He was smiling and all like somebody's favourite uncle but he didn't fool me. I guessed my parents would have told him I was at Tabby's, so I told him that too.

'Tabby. That'd be Tabitha Wentworth, Paul Wentworth's kid, right?'

'Right.'

'They still let her see you?'

'I – sure they do. Why not?'

'You had some trouble in school, didn't you?'

'What trouble – what d'you mean?'

'I think you know what I'm talking about, Zoe. I'm talking about Miss Moncrieff. About an imposition you did for her. I'm talking about brainwashing, Zoe.'

'Oh, that. Yeah, there was a bit of hassle about that. It's over now.'

'Is it?' he leaned forward, and he must be one of those guys who can't lean and smile at the same time because the smile faded.

'Is it over, Zoe? Don't some of the kids call you names? One name in particular? Don't they call you Chippy-lover?' His face got red as he spoke, and spit flew from his lips when he said Chippy. I shrugged. 'Sure. Some do. I take no notice.'

This seemed to make him sore. 'You take no notice? Your friends call you Chippy-lover and you take no notice? Don't you like to have friends, or what?' He was almost shouting.

'They're not my friends.' I spoke softly. He sat back and ran his tongue along his lip. 'Who are your friends, Zoe?'

'I dunno. I guess I don't have too many friends right now. Maybe I don't have any at all.' I wasn't about to give him names. The friend of a Chippy-lover is a Chippy-lover.

'Aw, come on.' The smile was back. 'It's not that bad, surely? You have at least one friend, dontcha?'

'Do I?'

'Why, sure you do. Tabby. She's your friend, right? You just spent the day with her.'

'We – talked. It's not like it was.'

'Ah.' His eyebrows went up. 'Are you surprised about that, Zoe?'

'How d'you mean?'

'Does it surprise you that friends might want to withdraw their friendship from a person who makes trouble in the community?'

'I don't make trouble.'

He nodded. 'Oh, yes you do, Zoe. When you wrote brainwashing on that imposition, you were suggesting that the State tells lies to the people.' He smiled, but his eyes didn't. 'Now you may be too young to realise this, but when somebody communicates an idea like that to others, it can do a lot of damage. People – some people – are liable to start picking at bulletins, looking for inaccuracies. And of course if you're looking too hard for something, you're liable to think you found it even if it's not there.'

I didn't say anything in answer to this. There was something wrong with it, but I couldn't put my finger on it, and anyway I was too nervous to argue with the lieutenant. They can put you in jail or take away your citizenship. If you lose your citizenship you have to leave your suburb and go live outside. You have no papers and no rights. Bang – you're a Chippy.

By this time I was getting really confused. Why was Pohlman interested in all this stuff about school? If they knew about Daz, why didn't he say so and get it over? Maybe he was enjoying himself, keeping me dangling. Or maybe –. I decided to find out once and for all. I looked at him.

'Lieutenant Pohlman, have I done something illegal?'

He smiled thinly. 'I don't know, Zoe. Have you?'

This threw me. I mean, you don't expect DS to admit it doesn't know. DS knows everything about everybody. It's the image. And it seemed this wasn't about Daz after all. I guess I sort of gulped with a mixture of surprise and relief, though I tried not to let the relief show.

'No,' I said. 'I haven't, so why am I being questioned?'

'You're not being questioned, Zoe.' He chuckled. 'You'd know it if you were. No – this is more in the way of a warning. A shot across your bow if you like. It's our way of saying we've got our eye on you, Zoe. You, and people like you. See, the trouble with your sort is, you don't know when you're well off. I mean, look around.' He made an expansive gesture. 'Silverdale, right? Silverdale's got everything. Space, beauty, climate, all the amenities. You got theatres, clubs, bars, stadia, pools, restaurants – every damn thing you can think of. You got nice houses and good roads and schools and colleges and a university. And you've got the most important thing of all, which is security. You're safe in Silverdale, Zoe. Safe and snug. Nothing can touch you. Nothing can hurt you. There are no hassles here. No problems.' He looked at me. 'Would you want to lose all that? Live outside? Is that what you want?'

I shook my head and he said, 'Then why are you making waves, kid? What do you want, that you don't have already?'

I shrugged and smiled. 'I want it for everyone.'

'Hah!' He got up and bent over with his face about an inch away from mine.

'Dreams, Zoe. Dangerous dreams. The world's the way it is, and you better pray it stays this way because you're one of the lucky ones.' He straightened and went to the door, pausing with his hand on the handle to look back at me.

'You wouldn't last a week out there,' he said.

○   □   ○

The cops weren't out the door before my parents started in on me. What did they want with you? What have you been doing, saying, thinking? Is that it, or are they coming back? Do you have to report anywhere, and if so when? Did you co-operate and were you polite?

I said, do we go straight into this second interrogation or do I get a cup of coffee in between?

I got the coffee, and then I told them everything Pohlman said. I was still feeling relieved they weren't on to Daz, but of course Mum and Dad didn't know anything about that, and when I got through Dad had a face on him like a man who's just been told he's gonna be fed to crocodiles.

'That's it,' he said flatly. 'They'll be watching us from now on. All of us, because we're suspect.' He looked at me. 'I hope you're satisfied, young lady. I hope you know what it is you've done here.'

'What has she done, Gerald?' At least Mum was trying to stick up for me. 'She wrote some words, that's all. Some foolish words, and the police have cautioned her. It's not the end of the world, for goodness sake.' She looked at me. 'She'll behave in future and every-thing'll be just like it was.'

Dad shook his head. 'No, it won't. That's not the way it works, Amanda, and you know it.' He got up and went to the window and stood with his hands in his pockets, looking out. 'Word gets around. Somebody says DS were at the Askew place last night, and some-body else says, Well, who'd have thought it – old Charlie. And before you know it they've got you figured for one of those FAIR guys or something and they stop putting business your way.'

'Fair guys?' I looked at Mum. 'What's a fair guy?'

Mum started to answer me but Dad broke in. 'Fair. F.A.I.R. It stands for Fraternal Alliance for Integration through Reunification. It's a proscribed organisation, Zoe. An illegal, underground outfit whose members believe the world'd be a better place if we tore down our fences and invited the Chippies to come share our lifestyle.' He laughed. 'They don't seem to realise our lifestyle would perish in about ten minutes after we did that, and most of us would perish with it. They're a bunch of spineless pinkos, and now folks're gonna think I'm one of 'em.'

'I'm sorry,' I said. 'I never even heard of FAIR. I didn't expect the cops to come running on account of a couple of words on a stupid imposition or I'd never have written them. And I can't believe such a small thing's going to affect you and Mum, anyway.'

He looked at me. 'You don't know, Zoe. You just don't understand. Those people out there are full of hate. They want what we've got, and these FAIR weirdos want to let 'em take it, even though it'll destroy everything we've worked for. It's Pohlman's job to sniff out those traitors, and I bet he thinks he's done just that.'

I didn't know what to say so I kept quiet, but I couldn't help wondering what was so wonderful about a society where the cops feel they have to watch what kids're writing, and a guy gets scared for his reputation and his livelihood just because of something his child did. Another thing I wondered was, what would Dad and Mum and Pohlman think if they knew I meant to take the tunnel into town tomorrow?

DAZ

She sends this crazy noat.

Half nine saterday nite i'm on my tod in the black diamond. Guy shoves past, damnear nock me over. i rekernise the crewboss. he don't say noffing but i find this paper in my pocket. i go in the bog 2 read it. shes only coming frou the tunnel tomorrow thats all. i groan. Zoe i sez, you barmy. i cant go 2 that tunnel no more. i got 1 toof missing plus 2 black eyes plus soar all over. i go near that tunnel 1 more tyme i'm ded.

i tear up the noat very littel. Frow it down the bog. i fink and fink but its no yuse i gotta go. i'm more scairtn i bin in my hoal lyfe but she be wayting down that tunnel 7 tomorrow nite so i gotta go.

Gudby world. so long our mam. sbin nise.

ZOE

I had spare batteries in case my torch gave out, and two enormous balls of knitting wool which I put in a plastic bag along with some of my cassettes. The story was that Tabby invited me over when I was there yesterday, but it nearly didn't work.

The visit from DS had really shaken my parents up. Mum had even peeped into my room around three that morning to check I hadn't slipped off somewhere, and all through Sunday if they couldn't see me they kept calling to ask what I was doing.

I got worried. Suppose they wouldn't let me out of the house. It seemed a distinct possibility. Daz would wait in the tunnel and I'd never show up, and he wouldn't know why. He'd think I got caught or lost underground or was lying in the dark with a broken leg or something. He might try to find me, and he wouldn't have the twine to guide him back.

The later it got the more nervous I felt. Daz had estimated the tunnel at around three miles long, and I'd planned on giving myself two hours to get through. I was meeting him at seven, so that meant I had to leave home around four-thirty. This was unusually early to be setting off for an evening with Tabby, and as the time drew near I wished I'd planned it differently.

Anyway, four twenty-five rolled around and my bag was packed and I couldn't stall any longer. 'Mum,' I called, coming downstairs. 'I'm going over to Tabby's to listen to music. I won't be late.' Mum was in the kitchen. I was halfway to the door when she yelled 'Hey – just a minute, young woman!' and appeared behind me with flour on her hands. Two seconds later Dad came out the den. I stood dangling my bag, looking from one to another.

'You're not going anyplace young lady,' said Dad. 'Not tonight.'

'Aw, but Dad – I promised.'

'Doesn't matter. You call Tabitha and tell her you won't be over after all 'cause your dad won't let you.'

'I can't tell Tabby that.'

'Well, you think of something then, because you're staying home and that's final.'

'Mum.' I turned to her, desperate, as you can imagine. 'Can't I just –.'

'You can just do as your father tells you, Zoe.'

This was it then. Disaster. I schlepped across to the phone with my heart in my socks. They stood watching me. I punched the Wentworth code and stood with the receiver in one hand and my bag in the other. I daren't let go that bag.

There were a couple of clicks, and then a high-pitched screech that damn near blew my head off. I jerked the receiver away from my ear.

'What's wrong?' This from Dad.

'Dunno. Funny noise.' He came over and took it and put it to his ear. 'Hmm. Fault on the line, maybe.' He re-dialled and got the same result. I clutched at this straw.

'Mum – I can't just not show up. Tabby's my best friend. I don't know what I'd do if she fell out with me.' My voice had a catch in it which wasn't entirely bogus.

Dad tried one more time and hung up. Mum said, 'She's right, Gerald – she can't just not show up.'

He looked at her, then at me. He shrugged. 'Okay,

okay.' He looked at his watch. 'It's four-thirty, Zoe. I want you back in this house at nine o'clock sharp. Sharp, d'you hear?'

'Yessir.' Never happen, I told myself, but it felt so good being off the hook I'd have promised anything.

O   ☐   O

It was scary in that tunnel even if you don't believe in ghosts and monsters and skeletons that walk, but the worst part was getting to the tunnel in the first place. It wasn't even properly dark yet, and I crept along expecting to be challenged any minute. DS could have the area staked out after Daz's narrow escape, and they might be watching me, anyway. Maybe they'd installed extra cameras or found the tunnel and sealed it. I didn't know what I'd say if some bouncer stopped me and searched my bag.

'Oh, I thought I'd just sit inside this old sewer pipe awhile and knit some covers for my cassettes. Pretty colour, isn't it?'

Anyway, I didn't meet anybody and I set off through the tunnel, letting out my wool and trying to remember what Daz had told me about the trip. I reached the foot of the rusty ladder at six thirty-five. Either I'd made good time in the conditions or it wasn't three miles.

I leaned on the ladder to wait. I thought I'd be smart and save my batteries by switching off. If you're not moving you don't need to see, right? Well, no, but it's just amazing the noises you hear, the stuff you imagine when you're alone in the dark. I kept switching on and

90

off, and in the end I gave up and left it on, jammed in a crack in the wall. It was better, but it didn't keep me from wondering if this was the right ladder.

He showed up four minutes early and I hardly recognised him, his face was such a mess. He was moving slow and he flinched and gasped when I squeezed him. 'What the heck happened to you?' I asked.

He told me. When he was through I said 'I'm sorry. This whole thing is so dangerous for you. You shouldn't have come.'

He laughed. 'And what if I hadn't? What would you have done – waited here till you died or what? Anyway, you know I can't stay away from you.'

It was good for a while after that. I forgot where we were, and the danger we were in. I forgot the time too, until we came out of a long clinch and he said, 'When d'you have to be home?' as though we were on a regular date or something. I held my wrist in the torchlight so I could see my watch. It was eight o'clock.

'I don't want to go back, Daz,' I said. 'I want to be with you all the time.'

'I know.' He held me. 'I want that too, but it can't happen and that's a fact. They've got us penned up in separate cages and there's no way out. We can't even see each other this way anymore.

I knew that. I'd been trying not to think about it. Now the realisation hit me like a truck. I broke away from him. 'It's not fair!' I cried. Fair, fair, fair, went the echo. 'Why should we live behind wire like something in a zoo?'

'Hey – sssh!' Daz caught hold of me, covered my mouth with hard fingers. 'They'll hear us up there.'

'Okay.' I shook my head and he took his hand away. 'But it's not right, Daz. It's not. People're just people, and when they love someone it's wrong to keep them apart.' I started to cry. I tried to stop myself but I couldn't. 'Who says, Daz? Who says we've got to live the way we do? Who are they, and what gives them the right?'

'Sssh.' He stroked my hair. For a husky guy he was surprisingly gentle. 'They're the government, Zoe, that's who they are. Nothing gives 'em the right – nothing can – but you see they don't need the right 'cause they've got the power. They've got it forever, too, 'cause only their friends get to vote.' He laughed. 'What d'you think Dred's about? Why d'you think guys and women get theirselves kilt all the time like that?'

I shook my head and he said, 'To break the power, Zoe. To get it away from them and give it to us.' I shook my head again.

'It doesn't work, Daz. All it does is cause more wire. More lights. More cops. There's got to be another way.'

'Yeah?' He looked down at me. 'What other way?'

'What about FAIR?' I murmured.

'FAIR?' He laughed. 'That bunch of nerds? What d'you think they're gonna do, Zoe?'

'They want us all to live together, don't they?'

'Oh, sure. And what do they do about it? I'll tell you. They have secret meetings. They print handbills and stick 'em on subway walls. Oh – and they like to be nice to Chippies, only not too nice or the lornorders might get suspicious.' He snorted. 'What good d'you think that'll do, Zoe?'

I shrugged. 'I dunno, Daz, but at least somebody's trying to do something. I wish –.'

'What?'

'I wish something would happen right now, or real soon. I don't want to wind up like Grandma, grieving for some guy she last saw eighty-eight years ago.'

We kissed then, and clung to each other but time was against us and we knew we were only prolonging the agony. I'm not going to go on about it. If you love someone – really love them, and if you can imagine how it'd feel to leave them with a very strong chance you'd never meet again – ever – then you've got it. And if you don't, and can't, it's no use my trying to put it into words.

I cried all the way back through the tunnel. All the way. Crying sounds real sad where there's echoing. It's the sound of total desolation. I didn't care much if I got out or lost myself down there in the dark, but I guess I must've followed the wool because after what seemed a long time I felt moving air on my wet cheeks and there I was, back in the cage.

I walked in home around ten-fifteen and it must've been obvious to my parents I'd been weeping. I walked in expecting to catch hell, but I guess they thought something had happened between Tabby and me, because they didn't say anything. When Mum asked was I all right and I burst into tears and ran up to my room, nobody followed.

Monday morning. School. Those used to be my two least favourite things. Now that Pohlman's visit had screwed everything up at home I was glad it was Monday. Glad to be out the house and biking, wrapped in mist, the shiny wet roadway to school.

Not that school was a million laughs, mind. There was still the name-calling and the ostracizing and all that. Even the teachers seemed cool toward me, though that could be just psychological.

No. The reason I wanted to be in school was Tabby. When you've only one friend you worry about her. You need to know where she is and what she's doing and if she's still your friend. You get a bit obsessive, in fact. And that's how I was about Tabby. You might think all this stuff with Daz would sort of push her into the background, and maybe it would have if he could be with me. As it was, the miles and the wire between him and me made me need her even more. I was afraid of this need. Afraid I might cling and that this clinging would smother her, drive her away. I wished she needed me.

What I wanted to do was tell her about Daz. I don't know if you've ever had a secret. A really heavy one. If you have you'll know what a relief it is to tell someone. And that's what I was going to do that Monday morning.

Except she wasn't there.

I searched the yard and the locker room and there was no sign of her. She wasn't in Mr Pawley's at registration. Right after registration I went along to the office and asked the secretary if anybody had called to say Tabby was sick. Mrs Corrigan gave me the sort of look everybody seemed to be giving me these days and said nobody had.

I went to my physics class. I've never liked physics and I couldn't concentrate. I made a stupid mistake and Mr Collins humiliated me in front of the class. Some of the kids had guessed what was bugging me and snickered, casting meaningful glances at Tabby's vacant seat. At breaktime I checked the office again, then went to the locker room.

Tabby's locker was next to mine. As I approached, I saw with relief that its door was open. That meant she'd arrived and was somewhere around. I hurried forward.

The locker was empty. Somebody had cleaned it out

and left the door wide open. They'd even torn down her Invaders picture. I checked around to make sure the thief hadn't just dumped everything on the floor, then made my way back to the office and rapped on the glass.

Mrs Corrigan slid the panel aside. 'Yes?'

'Tabitha Wentworth's locker, Mrs Corrigan. Somebody broke into it and took all her stuff.'

The secretary pursed up her lips and looked at me as though I was some kind of retard. 'No, Zoe Askew, they have not. Lawson has removed Miss Wentworth's property because she won't be returning to school.'

'Won't be −?' Lawson's the janitor. He only empties your locker if you died or something. 'Why?' I stared at her. My heart was kicking so hard my chest hurt. I gripped the counter. 'What's happened to Tabby, Mrs Corrigan? Where is she?'

'Don't shout, child.' She straightened some papers on her desk, not looking at me. 'I imagine your friend is at home, and if you take my advice you'll stay away from her.'

'Why? Is she sick? Is she going to die?'

Mrs Corrigan secured the sheaf of papers with a clip. 'I can tell you nothing more, Zoe. Tabitha Wentworth has left this school and will not return. And now if you'll excuse me I have work to do.' She reached out without looking at me and closed the panel.

The buzzer sounded end of break. I had an English class but I knew I was going to cut it. I had to. I'd die if I didn't find out what had happened to Tabby, and it was obvious nobody around here was going to tell me.

I sneaked off. That isn't hard to do when a school's got a thousand kids in it. I left my bike and just walked away across the playing field, keeping some out-buildings between me and the admin block, and got through a hole in the fence. I followed the fence along till I hit the road and headed for Tabby's place.

○ □ ○

I turned into Wentworth Drive and stopped dead. There was a cop at the bottom of Tabby's driveway. He was standing with his hands behind his back, looking across the street. My first thought was murder. Not long ago in a place called Summerhill a whole family had been murdered by the maid and the gardener, but surely there'd be more than one cop if it was something like that. Whole place'd be crawling. There'd be cars and an ambulance and the usual crowd of media ghouls.

Not murder, then. Some sort of accident? No, for the same reasons. And I could see there hadn't been a fire.

The house nearest to me – the corner house – looked quiet. The door was shut, and so were all the windows I could see. The garage door stood open and it was empty. No vehicle was parked in the driveway or at the curb. The cop was still looking in front of him. I set off up the driveway and was glad when I put the house between us.

I crossed the backyards. Five of them. I had to climb two fences, skirt three empty pools and crawl through a lot of wet bushes. I scared a cat and heard a dog and saw a Chippy maid in the window of house number four. She didn't see me.

Tabby was on the backporch, sitting on the step. She stayed there when I walked out of the shrubbery, and that's when I knew it must be bad. I went over and she squinted up at me and I saw she'd been crying.

'What're you doing here, Zoe? Why aren't you in school?'

I looked at her. 'I don't – what's up, Tabby? What's happened? They said you left.'

She nodded glumly. 'I did.'

'But why? Are your folks moving or what? You never said anything and I thought we were friends.'

She shook her head. 'You don't need friends like me, Zoe. I'd fade if I were you, before somebody sees you here.'

'What're you talking about, Tabby?' I hunkered down and gripped her shoulders. 'Why shouldn't I be here? Tell me.'

She shook her head, avoiding my eyes. Her mouth twisted up.'We are moving Zoe, but not through choice. We have to go tomorrow because –.' Her control snapped. She howled and threw her arms round me. 'They've kicked us out, Zoe. We can't stay here any- more.'

'I held her while she wept, her face buried in my shoulder. I stroked her hair as things started coming together in my mind.

'Your parents?' I said softly, 'They're in FAIR, right?'

She moved her head in mute affirmation. I didn't know what to say after that so I just held her. Little by little she grew quiet, and after a while she whispered, 'Go away, Zoe. There's a cop out front. If they find you here they'll think you're one of us.'

I hugged her. 'I am, Tabby. I know that now. I think I always was. That's been my trouble all along. What I can't understand is why your dad – I mean he's rich, important, all that. Why'd he want to change things, Tab?'

She shrugged. 'I don't know, Zoe. Conscience? I

97

mean, we all know what's right and what isn't, don't we? Even if we don't want to. I guess maybe he couldn't just sit back and enjoy all the good things he had, knowing there are people out there starving. And he's right, Zoe. They can kick us out and do whatever they want to do, but it won't alter the fact that he's right and they're wrong.'

'Listen!' I squeezed her and she lifted her head. 'I want to tell you something, Tabby.'

I told her everything. How Grandma'd always talked to me about the way it used to be. How I'd fallen for Daz that night at the Blue Moon. Our meetings and letters. Pohlman's visit. Everything. By the time I'd finished she'd dried her eyes and blown her nose and got herself pretty much together. She looked at me.

'I'm glad you told me, Zoe,' she said. 'I had no idea. But you certainly shouldn't be here when you know the police are watching you. They could decide to kick you and your parents out too, y'know.'

'I don't care, Tabby. I don't know if I want to go on living here anyway, now that you're going.'

She shook her head. 'Don't talk that way, Zoe. Silverdale's not so bad. You may be a little low on friends right now, but at least you get to eat every day and sleep in a warm bed nights.'

'Oh, Tabby – I'm sorry.' I'd been so wrapped up in my own little misfortunes I'd hardly spared a thought for the Wentworths' awful plight. I took her hand in mine. 'What'll you do, Tabby? Where will you go?'

'Oh.' She managed a watery smile. 'I didn't mean – it's not that bad, Zoe. Not for us. I mean, we won't starve or have to sleep in the woods or anything. We've got a place.'

I looked at her. 'What sort of place? Where?'

'A house. I don't know exactly where, but it's way out in the country. Dad started building it a long time ago, when he and Mum first got involved with FAIR.' She smiled again. 'Being rich and in real estate has its advantages. So you see – you won't have to imagine us cooking rats and possums over a woodfire and sleeping in the rain.'

'No.' I wrapped my arms round my knees. 'I'm glad about that, Tabby. But I still don't understand how it's gonna work for you. I mean, money and all that. Your dad won't be in real estate anymore.'

She shrugged. 'I don't know about any of that either, but I bet Dad's got it all figured. He's a real smart cookie, my dad.'

'I know.' I gazed down the backyard, wondering whose view this was going to be. 'I wish I was coming with you.'

'No, you don't. It sounds okay now, but I'm sure we'll have all kinds of problems out there. You stay and finish school and keep on thinking the way you do and maybe things'll change.'

She smiled. 'Maybe you'll be the one to change 'em, then you and Daz'll be together. And in the meantime there's always Grandma.'

I shook my head. 'Not always, Tabby. She's a hundred and four, y'know.'

'Yeah, well –.'

We sat looking down the yard, not saying anything. After a while the door opened behind us and Mrs Wentworth came out. Her eyes were red. I thought she might make me go away but she didn't. She set milk and cookies on the top step and left us to say our goodbyes.

I went home. School wasn't out yet, but I went home anyway, and you know it's just amazing the things you can discover by arriving home unexpectedly in the middle of the afternoon.

○ □ ○

Mum looked up from her magazine. 'Zoe. What're you doing home? It's only two thirty.' There was something in her voice that might be apprehension. I thought she was afraid I'd got myself into more trouble at school so I said, 'It's okay, Mum. It's not me this time, it's Tabby.' I thought she'd ask what about Tabby but she didn't. She said, 'It had to be today, didn't it? You never come home earlier than three-thirty and it had to be today.'

She sounded weary, resigned. This wasn't like her and fear flickered in me, deep down. 'What does that mean, Mum? What's so special about today that I shouldn't –.'

I broke off, listening. Footfalls above my head. Voices. Dad's and another, upstairs. I remembered there'd been an unfamiliar car at the curb when I came by just now. I looked at her. 'Who's upstairs, Mum? What's going on here?'

'Now, Zoe.' She got up. The magazine slid off her lap and she stepped on it and sort of tottered toward me with her arms out. 'You're not to get upset.'

She tried to take me in her arms but I shook my head and turned away. 'No, Mum. Don't do that. You've done something, you and Dad. Don't baby me. Tell me what it is.'

She dropped her arms and sighed. 'We meant to break it to you gently, dear. We didn't want you to find out this way, but how were we to know you'd come home in the middle –.'

'Tell me!' It was a shout. A scream. I couldn't help it. My fists were clenched so tight they were trembling and I was showing my teeth. I must've looked like a

100

wild animal and my mother recoiled with a small cry.

'Your father sold the house.'

Ah. I turned to the window, bracing my hands on the sill, resting my forehead on the cold pane which fogged with my breath. So that's it. I should've known. It's tainted for them now, this house. This formerly respectable house which is respectable no longer because the police were here. Because it could be under surveillance and people know. Ah, yes. That's the clincher. People know.

I closed my eyes. Behind me, Mum was silent. I heard Dad and the other guy come downstairs. The house door opened and they stood talking, keeping it low. I wondered what the guy'd made of my outburst a moment ago. Not that I gave a damn.

It wasn't just the house we'd be leaving. I knew that before the guy drove off and Dad came in and told me. Silverdale's not that big. You can't hide in it. You can't run away from something by moving house. What's known, if it's worth knowing, is known all over the suburb. You move and it'll follow you. No. The only way to wipe the slate clean and start over is to find another suburb. And that's what Dad had done. It was called Peacehaven, it was more than a hundred miles away and he'd bought a house there.

So. Goodbye Tabby, hometown, Grandma, Daz. Little Zoe's leaving you 'cause Daddy knows best. Daddy can't wait to get his little girl away to that nice, clean place where the past can't reach and there are no bad influences. Daddy's really looking forward to it.

Don't hold your breath, Daddy.

DAZ

leaving Zoe maid me feal so bad i coud dye. it woz late wen i got hoam but no yuse trying 2 sleap. Our mam in bed, so i tuck some doody stamps and some tucker stamps and trade them 2 a guy i know 4 peanuts. the idea is get smasht rite?

i dont go in that Blue Moon a longtyme now. i fink mebbe peeple remember how i get them Subbys away that tyme, plus Mick ther most nites. Mick see wot he done 2 my face he larf. tonite i dont care. its late and a long walk 2 that ovver club Black Diamond so i go in Blue Moon.

No trubble. Mebbe no 1 rekernise me wiv my mestup face but no 1 tork 2 me neever. i stand on my tod in a corna, nokking them back. this fing i'm drinking call a mixtup rite, cos 5 diffrent drinks init plus it gets you mixtup. Subbys call it lob otter miser. aniway i get 3 ov them mixtups down or 4 mebbe 5 and evryfing going rownd and rownd and i cant fink no more not even abowt Zoe and some 1 near me torking. i rekernise the voyce. i get my eyes lyned up and start my brain and its this guy wot beet up on me wiv Mick. hes torking 2 anovver guy. my lughoals not heering 2 gud plus my brain keep stopping but i heer Wentworf. Zoe frend call Wentworf. i moov up close 2 earwig.

i heer this. Lornorders kick Wentworf famly outer Silverdale Toozday. rich famly, bring lotsa gud stuff owt wiv em. 1 man 1 wumin 1 kid. thay come owt, this guy wayting 4 them wiv his mates. kill the Subbys nik ther stuff.

i fink, this kid Zoe frend. i gotta do somfing. i finish my mixtup, leeve. owtside i cant wolk 2 gud i hit 1 howse bounce of hit anovver howse fall down larfing, sleap.

ZOE

'Oh hello, Zoe. I've been expecting you.' Grandma moved aside so I could come in, and closed the door behind me. 'Go through. I'll get coffee.'

'I didn't come for coffee, Grandma.'

'I know, child, but a good cup of coffee never hurt, and waiting for it'll give you time to cool off. Sit down.'

I sat but I didn't cool off. The way I was feeling, that wouldn't have been possible. I gazed out the window, seeing nothing, picking at the knee of my jeans.

Grandma brought in the coffee, poured and sat down. 'They told you, then?'

'Only because they had to. I came home early, caught 'em selling the place. Otherwise they'd probably have told me on the way to the airport.'

'I don't think that's quite fair, dear.'

'Fair?' I looked at her. 'What's fair got to do with it' Grandma? D'you think it's fair to take someone away from everything they've ever known without even talking to them about it first?'

She shook her head. 'I don't, and I said so to your mum and dad, but they thought they were handling it right.'

'Well, I'm not going, so there.'

'Now, don't be silly, dear. Your parents have decided to move, and since you are not yet old enough to look after yourself you have no choice but to go with them.'

'I could stay here with you.'

She shook her head. 'No, Zoe, you could not, for three reasons. One – your parents would never agree. Two – I have only the one little bedroom. And three – I'm a hundred and four years old and it takes me all my time to take care of myself.'

'I'd help you. I could clean the apartment and cook and all like that. I'm not a little kid.'

'Zoe.' She leaned forward and took my hands in hers. 'I know how you feel but it's no use – the decision's been made. I don't like it any more than you do but we're not in control, child.' She smiled and squeezed my hands. 'You'll make new friends, wait and see. Once you're there, it won't be nearly as bad as you think.'

'Oh, Grandma. You're just saying the sort of stuff all adults say to kids. I thought you were different. You always used to be.'

She smiled, but it was a sad smile. 'What did you want me to say, Zoe? Run away? Leave Silverdale in the middle of the night, go be a Chippy? Is that what you expected?'

I nodded. 'That, or something like it, yes.' I looked into her eyes. 'Why shouldn't I run away, Grandma? I could go to Daz. He'd look after me.'

'Daz?'

'The guy I met. You know – the one I told you about?'

She nodded. 'He got in touch?'

'We've met up, Grandma. Twice. He's been here in Silverdale and I've been out.'

'Oh, Zoe!' She squeezed my hands so hard her rings dug in. 'That is so dangerous, dear. If DS knew you were fraternising with someone from outside they could make you leave Silverdale – your dad and mum too – and live as Chippies for the rest of your lives. Did you know that?'

105

I nodded. 'I know. The Wentworths leave tomorrow.'

'Paul Wentworth?'

'Yes. And his wife and my best friend Tabby. They're in FAIR.'

'How come you know about this, Zoe?'

'Tabby told me.'

'Ah. Huh. Well, that's a pity. Just when we –.' She let go my hand and sat back. 'I can see now why you're so upset, you poor thing. First your best friend, then your home, and all in a day, too. And Daz, of course.'

She didn't say anything after that. She folded her knotty, thin hands in her lap and sat looking at them. I drank my coffee, watching her over the rim of the cup. Maybe I wouldn't have to move to Peacehaven after all.

It was nothing like that. Later, I was to find out she'd been brooding about something far more important than my problem, but at the time I thought she was thinking up a plan. You can imagine my disappointment when she looked at me and said, 'I wish there was some way I could make all of this easier for you, Zoe, but there isn't.'

I went home and found my parents packing. Dad said 'We leave Friday.' I didn't say anything.

I had my thoughts, though.

DAZ

Monday i woak up erly. You sleap all cold nite on crack stoans you wake up erly 2. my hed banging plus i feal pukey but i remember i got somfing 2 do.

Firs gorra gerra gun.

Easy. Dred got moast of the guns but i know wear is 1. our Del put 1 gun under the flor at hoam. after thay topt him sumtymes wen our mam owt i tuck it owt luck at it. fink, sumday i kill 1 Subby wiv this 4 our Del. This gun bilong 2 Dred but our Mam dont know its ther and i never turnd it in.

i ronik innit? me keeping this gun 2 kill 1 Subby now i'm gonna yuse it 2 save 3.

Nex fing. wear this guy gonna hambush them Subbys? Not near Silverdale 4 shor. Start shooting near Silverdale, fans com shoot you. Moas kickout Subbys hed 4 town, luck 4 old howse 2 liv in. So. This hambush probly sumwear between Silverdale and town. gorra get myself hid tonite, foller the guy. i hoap hes only got 4 mates – our Del gun got 5 bullits.

i cleenup, get my hed down 2 be fresh 4 the job. wear you going sez our mam wen i'm leeving arownd 9. No wear Mam i sez. No yuse her worrying. i can worry enuff 4 2.

ZOE

I didn't go to school Tuesday. My parents thought I did, but I didn't see why I should expose myself to the sort of hassle I'd been getting there, for the sake of three more days. And anyway I had some thinking to do.

First I thought I'd go round to Tabby's, maybe see her one more time, but I decided the Wentworths'd have enough to do without me hanging around, plus I didn't know if I could stand another of those goodbyes. So I went to the park and sat on a bench by the pond where there are ducks but very few people this time of year.

I'd been awake most of the night trying to decide what to do. I'd tried to image what it'd be like to be a hundred miles away from Daz, knowing for certain we were never going to meet again and not even able to communicate through notes. I couldn't do it. I thought about Tabby, and I thought about Grandma. Mum had told me she and Dad had offered to take Grandma to Peacehaven too but she refused, saying she liked her own place, that her life was in Silverdale. I've always loved Grandma, and the thought of being way up there in Peacehaven without her to talk to was more than I could bear. So, with dawn in my window I decided that whatever happened I would not go to Peacehaven, and with that I fell asleep.

It's easy to make brave vows when you're tucked up snug in bed. There, dream and reality get mixed up even if you're awake. In the grey light of morning, huddled in my coat under that steely cold sky it seemed a lot harder. I was still determined to do it, but now I was having to face up to the difficulties, and there were many.

First, I had to get out of Silverdale. That may not sound so hard but I don't drive, and they don't let you walk out. There was the tunnel, of course, but I didn't dare contemplate using that when DS might be watching. There'd be no point getting away and then being killed by Dred for betraying their route into the suburb.

Then if I did get out, how would I live? There was no work out there, and I was too young to qualify for the government foodstamps and clothing vouchers most Chippies exist on. I'd be relying on Daz, but what if he couldn't help? I was beginning to realise I knew nothing about his circumstances, except he had a mother and they lived in the highest apartment block in Rawhampton. Would Daz's mother be prepared to feed me? Would she be able to? And anyway, why should she?

And then there's Mum and Dad. Okay, so they haven't been all that supportive toward me lately, but they're my parents and I love them. Once I go through that wire, I've lost them forever. With me outside, it won't matter whether they're here in Silverdale or a hundred miles away in Peacehaven, I'll never see them again. And that goes for Grandma too, of course. If I run away, I'll be leaving her far more finally than if I went with Mum and Dad. Flights and freeways link all suburbs, no matter how remote, but nothing spans the yawning chasm that lies between Veezaville and Chippyland.

After a while I got chilled sitting on the bench and some little kids came to feed the ducks, so I got up and went off to try to find out where the trash trucks work on Wednesdays.

DAZ

i hed norf. Owt past wear the tunnel is 2 wear the
bildings fin owt and all fall down. no 1 livs hear. 2 near
Silverdale. 2 near lornorders but gud place 4 hambush.
Kickowt Subbys moasly come here firs, spend the nite.
i get down behynd a bit ov wall, Del gun handy, wait.

4 a longtyme noffing. i start finking mebbe i got the
rong place plus i'm ded cold then i heer som littel fing
lyke some 1 kick a stoan. i luck owt and i see 2 guys
coming lyke mooving shadders, sept shadders dont hav
ryfels, rite? Thay creep rite by me. i luck 2 see ovvers
com but no 1 else. i'm glad thers oanly 2. Thay past me
and i foller littel bit norf littel bit norf til thay fynd a
spot thay lyke. Thay all the tyme torking so dont heer
me. thay hyde in 2 ruins, 1 this syde the street 1 the
ovver but torking acrost lyke on a picnic or somfing. i
fink if Cal seen em he larf or mebbe shoot em in the
mouf. i get behynd the 1 wot don me over. i never fyred
a gun but coudn miss from hear.

we settel down, wait 4 morning. longtyme. i seen 1
rat and 1 fin dog plus i heer a lot ov rabbit witch it
coms from the guys moufs.

i'm frozen. glad wen i seen it start 2 com lite. gorra
be careful now thogh or som 1 spot me.

waiting waiting waiting. Sunup now but no warmf
init. no Subbys neever. i get in payshent, fink wy wait
4 Subbys? oanly 2 ov em. shoot em now get it don wiv.

boaf guys worrid now torking acrost the street wear

ar thay? wy thay not com? lucking norf, never luck behynd. i pickup Del gun, my fingers feal stiff wiv cowld plus i got the shayks, speshly my hand. i never kilt a guy bifoar. i lift the gun, breev in hold my breff consentrait fink how this guy neal on my back wile Mick ram my face in the muck. no shayks now. sqeez. Bang!!! Del gun jumps. the guy face hits the wall in front ov him noyze lyke splitting happel and he slydes down leeving blod on the brix. no sownd. jus slyding down and this littel hoal lyke belly button in his back.

wen i fire, this ovver guy yell owt Pete – hey Pete wot you shooting at? i duck down say noffing. Pete say noffing 2 – firs tyme in his lyfe probly. the guy yell owt again Pete hey Pete. i stay hid. after a minit stoans rattel and futsteps running. i luck owt, see the guy running souf lyke the clappers.

Noffing more 2 tel. i tutch Pete wiv my foot. he wont neal on no 1 elses back. i wolkit acrost the street, luck norf. No Subbys. Mebbe thay dint get kickowt after all. mebbe old Pete got it rong. i bet he fink so.

i go souf, hoam 4 brake fast.

Wear you bin our Daz, sez Mam.

no wear Mam, i sez.

thats jus wear you sed you was going, she sez.

shes dry, our mam.

ZOE

Another sleepless night, and I must've changed my mind a hundred times as the hours dragged by.

Put yourself in my place. You love your parents but you've decided to leave forever without even saying goodbye. You're gonna do it tomorrow, so this is your last night in the bed you've slept in all your life. You're going out under a trash truck, and any one of four things might happen. You might be seen getting under, in which case the whole thing's blown. You might succeed in getting under, but be spotted at the gate. If that happens the crew dies and they put you away someplace you'll never get out of. If you make it through the gate you might lose your hold as the truck speeds along the freeway, in which case you're dead. Or you might succeed and find yourself without food or shelter in a bleak and alien world.

Would that help you sleep?

Anyway, morning comes and I have to act normal. I feel like the condemned guy must feel, eating a breakfast that'll never get digested because in less than an hour he'll be dead. Unreal's the word, I guess. Or detached.

There we sit, the three of us, eating cornflakes, as usual, and Mum says something like, 'I've packed everything we won't need before Friday. Have you called the telephone company yet?'

And Dad says, 'I'll do it from the office, first thing.' He's sold the business and is tying up loose ends.

Mum looks at me. 'Be sure to remind Mrs Corrigan about your file, Zoe. They'll want it at your new school.'

'Okay, Mum,' I say. My breakfast's choking me but when will I eat cornflakes again?

Dad's leaving. To keep from bursting into tears I think about how he sold our home without even telling me. I grip my spoon and stare into my bowl and keep thinking about that till the sound of his car fades away. Even then I have to blink back some tears but my head's down and Mum doesn't notice.

I mumble that I'm not hungry, push my bowl away and leave the kitchen. In my room I sit on my bed (last time here) and weep. I do it as quietly as I can, though my parents never come in without asking. I feel I could cry forever, but I have to make it look like I'm going to school.

I pick up my stuff and go downstairs. My eyes are red but that's okay – Mum knows I'm upset we're leaving. She's doing the dishes. I can hear her at the sink. I can't go in there. I know if I do I'll abandon my plan. I conjure up a picture of Daz, put on my anorak with the big pockets, call out, 'Bye, Mum,' and leave (forever) through the front door.

Wednesdays, the trucks work the commercial section. I pedal that way. It's eight forty-five and lots of other people are going that way too, but none of them are kids. There's no school near the commercial section. I feel conspicuous. If Pohlman's having me tailed they'll pick me up for sure. At the first intersection I turn off and make for one of the supermarkets. Crossing an overgrown vacant lot I dump my bike and books and other school stuff. It feels like a decisive step. No turning back.

There was this story in all the papers oh – two years ago. A Chippy, Dred fanatic, rode into Fairlawn Suburb in broad daylight under a trash truck. Suicide mission.

113

Sprayed a shopping mall with machinegun fire till the bouncers cut him down. Sixteen, seventeen people died. Anyway the papers printed a diagram showing how the guy rode the truck, and that's how I'm going out.

In the supermarket I buy stuff I can carry in my pockets. Stuff Chippies can't get, or can't get easily, like cigarettes and fancy soap and coffee. I buy a lipstick and a compact and a tin of Germolene and some aspirin and a box of candy. I get butter and cheese and salami. I make my selection thoughtfully, with Daz's mother in mind. It's a sort of bribe. I spend quite a lot of my savings but I hang onto some too, aware that the most precious commodity of all out there is cash.

I check out at nine thirty and the road to the commercial section is a lot quieter. All of the buildings that make up the section are similar – long, low structures of glass and concrete, severe and functional but well spaced with smooth lawns and tidy flowerbeds between. Today the flowerbeds have that depressing, washed-up look you get in early November so they match my mood exactly.

I see a trash truck right away, but the sound the trash makes going in tells me it's still almost empty, with a long way to go. I walk on, taking care to steer well clear of the block where Dad has his office.

I find what I'm looking for at ten past ten. The truck is parked up between two factory units and the four man crew is leaning on a wall, taking a break. I walk past. The guys are smoking, chewing the fat. None of them looks in my direction. Beyond their line of vision I turn left and walk toward the door of the building, hoping nobody's watching me through the windows of tinted glass. Instead of going to the door I turn left again and walk along the front of the factory to the corner. Here I flatten myself against the wall and take a peek. If DS are watching now, they'll have me for sure. Maybe I'm half hoping they will.

The truck's about four metres away, between me and the crew. By looking under the vehicle I can see their feet. I glance around. A pickup is cruising up the street. I lean on the wall and pretend I'm fixing a hangnail till it goes by. Then I take a deep breath and walk to the truck, praying no crewman sees my feet, and duck under. In the shadow I crouch motionless, my hair touching the caked, oily dirt under the truck. If DS have been watching, surely now's the moment they'll strike? Seconds pass and there's no shout, no pounding feet. Am I relieved or disappointed? I dunno. I breathe out slowly, looking for the brackets it showed in that diagram, hoping the crew's break won't end just yet. I spot them – eight flat strips of steel which fasten the truck's side-guards to the chassis. They cross at forty-five degrees the right angle between the side-guard and the underneath of the truck. There are four of them on each side. They're about three feet apart, and I find I can easily wrap my arms round one and swing my legs up through the next so that the strip is hooked behind my knees. The trouble is that this leaves me very close to the side, so that anybody glancing between the slats of the side-guard will be sure to see me hanging like a sloth. Still, it's a good secure position and the best I can manage.

I dangle. If you think I'm not scared, you're crazy. I'm terrified. It's not the danger of being spotted, so much as the thought of what it'll be like when the truck starts moving. I mean okay, it's been done before, but that guy knew he was going to die anyway and I'm no Dred fanatic.

Presently, the crew decides to move, and I'm in luck. We've no more calls to make. The vehicle bounces a bit but we're headed straight for the nearest gate. My butt's clearing the cement by about four inches and there's a terrific sense of speed. To take my mind off this I turn my head to the right and peer through the slats. We've cleared the commercial section and are passing through a leafy residential part. Pedestrians walk dogs and push strollers within six feet of me but nobody looks at the truck. I pray to God to send us no red lights, and we get none.

For some reason, now that it's actually happening I don't feel nearly so bad as I did earlier. Adrenalin, I guess.

At the gate there's no hassle at all. I'm amazed. We stop, but the bouncer doesn't even leave his kiosk. He just yells something to the crewboss who yells something back, the pole goes up and we're through. We cruise along the freeway. I'd pictured myself, if I ever got this far, clinging on for dear life as the jolting flung me this way and that, threatening to break the tenuous hold of my aching arms on some greasy gismo. Forget it. The jolting's minimal till we turn off the freeway, and it's only minutes to the dump from there.

At the dump three of the men get out and walk off, leaving the crewboss to dump the trash. While he's doing that, leaning out the cab and looking back, I roll out on his blind side and get down behind a mound. It stinks, but I'm out.

And that's how easy it is. Of course, they're not looking for people breaking out. I mean, what Subby in her right mind would choose to be a Chippy?

DAZ

i dint get no sleap that nite even thogh i wos nackert. 2 worid, see. that Pete 1 ov Cal guys and i kiltim. also it com reel cowld and the wind blue the polifeen sheat down of the broken windo. i after get up and fixit and wen i go back 2 bed i cant get warm even wiv 2 coats over.

Wensday morning our Mam fynd all the tucker stamps gon. ear our Daz she sez wears all the bleedin stamps. i canot tel a lye our Mam i sez (not much i cant) it wos me.

she giv me el. i after take it. i feal roten alreddy and she maykit wors. owm i spos 2 fead the 2 ov us wivowt stamps she sez. dunno Mam i sez. no she sez neever do i.

no brake fast, plus she send me owt in the cowld 2 deel stamps or tucker. How do i know wear is deelas Wensday morning? i take Del gun witch it all i got to deel and hang abowt, aster cupple guys, finely pickup this hardloaf bred and lengf ov sossidge witch the sossidge probly dog. After handover Del gun and the guy wont frow in no coffee neever the tite git. Me and Mam eat the bred and sossidge and i dont find no collar init witch is 1 big serprize.

bigger serprize coming thogh.

ZOE

When the truck moved off I stayed down. With the actual escape behind me my mind was free for the first time to contemplate the enormity of the step I had taken, and I found myself overwhelmed by a combination of emotions, the strongest of which were regret, sheer disbelief and rising panic. It was as much as I could do to stop myself jumping up and running after the truck, begging to be taken back. I stuffed my handkerchief in my mouth, closed my eyes and fought for the control which alone could help me now.

I don't know how long I stayed there. I know that gradually I became aware that I was terribly cold, and that the cry of gulls was everywhere. I pulled the wadded handkerchief from my mouth, wiped my face with it and thrust it into a pocket with the aspirin and the cigarettes.

I was shaking. Stop it, I said to myself. Stop this right now, Zoe, or you're finished. You're here. This is real. Regret's worse than useless and panic'll get you killed.

I raised myself a little and looked over the mound. Three, four hundred yards away some guys were working, sorting stuff into piles. A little way beyond them was a track, and beyond that was open ground, covered with weeds and scrub. There seemed to be no fence round the dump – nothing to stop me getting up and just walking away. I didn't do it, though, because I had no idea what the guys' reaction would be if a

Subby kid suddenly materialised among them. What would they do – kill me? They might. Nobody'd ever know. They could belt me over the head and make a hole and plant me and I'd be gullfeed – part of the dump.

I looked around. Off to my left was where the trucks checked in – a little hut beside a muddy track. As I watched, a truck drew up and a man came out of the hut and stood, talking to the driver. Not that way, then. Directly behind me were great drifts of garbage. It was impossible to know what lay beyond them, so I looked to my right. A track marked the boundary of the dump in that direction too, but it must be at least a quarter of a mile away. There were no vehicles, though, and no people I could see. I was in jeans and anorak. If I got up and walked that way without hurrying, maybe nobody would notice me. One thing was certain – if I stayed where I was I'd either be discovered or I'd freeze to death. I stood up and started walking.

Nobody shouted. The guys who were sorting went right on doing it, and the man by the hut continued to talk to the driver. I plodded on with my head down in imitation of the Chippy's dejected gait. I was walking away from the city but that was all right – once off the dump I could circle round, and it was only eleven thirty.

I made it to the track with muddy shoes, but no trouble. I began to circle the dump clockwise, watching out for people. When I saw the little hut in front of me I made a detour through the scrub, not returning to the track till I'd left it way behind. When I'd walked a half-circle there was a road, half choked with weeds, which seemed to go toward the city. I turned on to it and after that I didn't see anybody for quite a while. I plodded on, looking for the tallest block in town.

○   □   ○

It's a bit vague, the tallest block in town. If I'd had any idea this was going to happen the last time I saw Daz, I'd have got the street and his apartment number. And if I'd had more time I'd have done some other things, too. I'd have worked out a way to take some of my warmest clothing with me for a start. As it was I only thought how I'd need both hands free to hold on to that truck, and so I'd brought nothing that wouldn't go in my pockets. I could've worn some extra things as a way of getting them out but I hadn't. In short, this had to be the worst-organised expedition ever mounted.

The weeds thinned out as I approached the city. I was passing between broken buildings now, and I began to see people. First there were some little kids in the ruins. I guess ruins make neat places to play if you're a kid. This bunch were standing in a ring, laughing and poking with sticks at something on the ground. I didn't look their way because I didn't want to attract their attention, but as I drew level one of them, a tiny, dirty-nosed girl called out, 'Hey missus, come see what we got.' I pretended not to hear, but then the others started calling and I was scared their noise might bring people so I went over.

It was a dead man. They'd found a dead man and filled his nose, mouth and one ear with twigs and grass stems. They'd removed his boots. A little boy was wearing them round his neck. If this'd been Silverdale I'd have shooed the kids away and called a cop. Here, I was at a loss. I said, 'This poor man is dead. You should tell somebody – an adult, not be fooling around like this.' They gazed at me as if I was something from another galaxy, and the biggest boy – the one with the boots – eyed me shrewdly and said, 'He's ours, missus. We found him. You wanna buy his doodies?

Doodies is Chippy for clothes. I shook my head.

'Boots?' He lifted them so I could see the soles. 'Good boots for your fella. Goin' for peanuts.'

'I – I don't have –.'

'Stamps, then. Gimme stamps.'

I'd been about to say I had no fella. He thought I had no cash. I shook my head again. 'Look, I don't want – you shouldn't be doing this. This is a corpse. You can get diseases. All sorts of nasty things. What would your parents –?' I didn't know what I was saying, really. I just wanted out of there.

The boy peered at me through red-rimmed, narrow eyes. 'You – you Subby, encha?'

His companions regarded me now with a fresh interest. I nodded. 'Yes. That is, I was. Not anymore. I ran away. Do you know a boy – a man, called Daz?'

He eyed me scornfully, ignoring my question. 'Ran away?' He laughed, jeeringly. 'Gerraway, missus. Subbies don't run away. You kickout, right?'

I shook my head. 'No. I ran away. D'you know a man called Daz? He wears a black leather jacket.'

'Black leather granny! You kickout, encha? Wanna place? Gimme peanuts, I show you a place. Good place. Dry.' He grinned, thrusting out a grubby palm.

I shook my head once more and turned away. Behind unbroken cloud the sun was falling westward. I knew if I didn't find Daz before dark something would happen to me. Watching these kids had convinced me of that. They were just little kids, but they looked and behaved like rats. Thin, darting, glitter-eyed rats. If they'd known what was in my pockets I think they'd have killed me for it, small as they were. I hurried away and their cries pursued me. Kickout, they shrilled. Kickout, kickout, kickout.

○　　□　　○

I was now approaching the centre of Grandma's beloved Rawhampton, or what was left of it. I'd spotted a very tall building some minutes before and was hurrying toward it in the hope that it would turn out to be Daz's block. I'd seen a bit of the town from Ned Volsted's car the night we went chippying, but it'd been practically dark, and anyway you don't see things all that well from a car. That brief glimpse certainly hadn't prepared me for the panorama of desolation which now unfolded around me.

The streets were cracked and broken and littered with every sort of debris. Long puddles of foul, stagnant water lay in gutters clogged with filth. Here and there sat the rusting carcasses of cars and trucks, completely stripped and without their wheels. Some were evidently in use as dwellings, because I saw makeshift curtains strung over glassless windows and signs of life behind them. And these weren't the worst places. Among the rubble of smashed and burned-out buildings, people had made shanties out of crates and plastic sacks and cardboard boxes. Little fires smouldered before some of these and listless children huddled in the smoke, poking the flames with sticks. There was an unpleasant smell, strong in some places, faint in others, but always there.

I'd just begun to think every building in the city must be derelict when I came to a row of little shops. Plate glass windows gleamed dully behind heavy-gauge wire mesh, and there were crudely painted signs above. One said **RUDY'S DOODIE'S – bought and sold – cash stamp's xchange.** Another said **TUCKER – savage dog on gard.** A small, home-made handcart stood outside this shop and in the cart, swaddled in rags, lay a baby.

As I gazed around, the enormity of the step I had taken began to dawn and I wondered whether, if I were to run all the way back to the dump and get under a truck, I might get back into Silverdale before anyone realised I'd gone.

It was pure fantasy and I knew it, but a sort of panic was growing in me and my mind was searching frantically for something to keep it from snapping. I knew if I dwelt on my situation now I'd start screaming, and that if I screamed forever it wouldn't change a thing. With a terrific effort I tore my mind away from thoughts of undoing what could never be undone, and walked on into how things really are.

○   □   ○

How things really are. Daz had told me he lived with his mother in an apartment, and like you do I'd formed pictures in my mind of what I imagined his mother and the apartment would look like. They were nothing fancy, these imaginary pictures. I'd seen apartment blocks and a selection of their inhabitants through the windows of Ned's car, and of course I'd been fed all my life with stories about how Chippies live. I knew I wasn't about to walk into some antiseptic glass palace and meet a beautifully turned-out matron whom Daz would introduce as his mother, but I'd no idea how bad it would actually be.

From the outside, the block was like the ones I'd seen. There were the usual damp-stained walls and broken, boarded-over windows, and the usual knot of dirty, red-eyed kids round the doorway. It was when I got through the doorway things started to get heavy.

I mentioned a smell before – the one that was strong in some places and faint in others. Well, that was the first things that hit me, and I do mean hit. I was in a dim lobby with a cement floor and rough plaster walls that were covered with graffiti. In front of me was a flight of cement stairs and an elevator. I could tell by just looking at it the elevator hadn't worked in a long, long time. The floor felt sticky under my shoes and there were puddles and piles of trash in corners. I nearly gagged on the smell. The kids, squealing and chattering, had come in after me. Their voices echoed in the bleak lobby and they plucked at my clothes.

'Daz,' I asked. 'Does Daz live here?' A small boy jerked his head toward the stairs. 'free up.'

'Thanks.'

The half-landing windows were boarded up so the stairway was dark and I kept stepping on squashy things I couldn't see. There seemed to be four apartments on the first floor, but only one had a door, so maybe the others were unoccupied. On the next floor two apartments had doors. A fierce-sounding dog threw itself against the inside of one just as I was passing.

All of the third-floor apartments had doors. I stopped by one that had the number eleven painted on it, and knocked. Some of the kids had followed me up. They stood on the stairs, watching me through rusty iron rails. I heard footsteps, and a voice, suspicious, called, 'Yeah?' I knew that voice.

'It's me, Daz. Zoe.' A bolt scraped, the door flew open and we were in each other's arms.

We were in a little hallway that had the same cement floor as the landing outside, only cleaner. Not clean, but cleaner. The walls had once been yellow, but damp must've got in, and now the paint was curled and blistered and flakes of it lay on the floor. There was a smell like toadstools. Four doors led off this hallway, one in front of me and three on my left. The one straight ahead was open and led to a kitchen. When Daz closed the outer door the only light came from there.

Daz took my hand and led me to the last door on the left. As he opened it he called out, 'Hey, Mam, look – we got a visitor.' The forced cheerfulness was transparent and I felt like I was walking into an ogre's lair.

Scattered across the floor were bits and pieces of matting and threadbare carpet. Apart from these the room contained only an iron stove whose chimney went out through a window, and two chairs, one each side of the stove. The chairs were saggy, colourless armchairs and in one of them sat a woman who might have been made to match. With a son like Daz she couldn't have been much more than forty-five, but she looked at least seventy. She was wearing a lumpy green cardigan over a black, turtleneck sweater and a long grey skirt with a ragged hem. Her thin legs were bare except for blue ankle socks and her feet were encased in what looked like a man's broken boots. Grey hair hung in greasy rat-rails to her shoulders. White bony fingers gripped the armrests of her chair and she gazed at her son with lustreless eyes.

'Visitor? What you on about, our Daz? Who is it?'

'I'm Zoe, Mrs –.' I broke off. I didn't know her name. I'd run away from home to be with someone whose name I didn't even know.

Daz said, 'This is Zoe, Mam. She's a – she's from Silverdale. She'll be staying here awhile.'

'Staying?' The woman leaned forward. 'A Subby lass, staying here? Have you gone barmy, lad? D'you want to get us both topped? How'd she get out of Silverdale anyway?'

'Under a trashtruck,' I said. 'I rode out under a trashtruck.'

'Aye, and what you done, that's what I'd like to know. What they want you for in Silverdale, eh?'

'Nothing. I haven't done anything, Mrs –. I ran away to be with Daz.'

'Daz? What's our Daz got to do with you?' She looked at her son.

'Only one reason Subbies run. They done something, see? DS wants 'em. She stays here, place'll be crawling with lornorders 'fore you can turn round. Get her out of here, son. Get rid of her.'

Daz looked from me to her. 'I can't, Mam. Where's she supposed to go – out on the street? Anyway, I love her.'

'Love?' The woman laughed wheezily. 'You telling me you fell for a Subby girl after what they did to our Del? Forgot, did you?'

He shook his head. 'No, Mam. I didn't forget. I've never forgotten our Del, have I? Wanted to join Dred

126

and get 'em back, only you weren't that keen, were you?'

'Huh! Wouldn't have you now, though, would they? Subby-lover they'd call you, and they'd be right. Anyway she can't stay here. I want no raids on this house, we've trouble enough.'

I know what you're thinking. You're thinking this old lady's hospitality stinks, but she was right. They execute Chippies who harbour fugitives or kidnap people, and I'd come here thoughtlessly, expecting to be taken in. I realised now what I'd done, and if there'd been anywhere else for me to go – anywhere at all – I'd have walked out, but there wasn't. Death was waiting outside, and so I had to stand there while Daz and his mother fought over me.

In the end they compromised. The old lady said that since it was dark now I'd better stay till morning. Daz winked at me. I guess he thought his mother would relent tomorrow and everything would be fine. I wasn't so sure.

With that and missing my family, I'd have spent a lousy night if they'd put me in a feather bed. A damp mattress on the floor and a coat to cover me left me no chance. My feet were like chilled mutton and I think I cried all night.

Barraclough, their name is. The old lady told me at breakfast. She's different in the mornings because that's when she pops her pill. She's got something Chippies call the dulleye, which I guess is depression, and she's on pills for it.

Breakfast was at 8 a.m. It was hot, watery coffee and hard bread. Daz and his mother dunked their bread in the coffee so I did too. Afterwards Daz told me the bread was a special treat because I was there – usually they just have the coffee.

They don't talk over breakfast, the Barracloughs. I sat there trying to eat wet bread without slurping, saying Darren Barraclough over and over in my head. Darren Barraclough. I like it. I think it has a ring to it. I needed to find things I liked that morning.

They don't talk over breakfast, but we talked straight after. The old lady's pill saved me from having to leave right away but it didn't blunt her sense of reality. She started asking me questions. Did my parents know anything about Daz. What did I say to them when I left the house. Had I left a note. What time yesterday would they have started to worry. When would they have known I was definitely missing. What would they do then. Had I relatives or friends in Silverdale I might be with. In other suburbs. Would they get the police in right away. What did I think they'd think had happened to me.

I did my best to answer. She and Daz knew the authorities would be looking for me, and that sooner or later they'd widen their search to include the city. I said, 'The city's a big place to find one person in. Surely if I stay indoors till they get tired looking it'll be okay?'

Daz shook his head. 'You were seen, Zoe, yesterday. The kids you told me about, and them downstairs. Others. You were dirty from the dump but even the little kids had you sussed. Lornorders pay for information and there's a lot of hungry people out there. Soon as the law comes sniffing around, someone'll finger you.'

'Then what can we do, Daz? What do I do? I don't

want to bring the police down on you, but I don't know any place outside of Silverdale other than this.'

'I know. Listen. I have to go out for a while. See a guy.' He stood, pulling on his jacket. 'I've got an idea but I don't know if I can swing it. You stay here with Mam and don't even stick your nose outside.' He turned in the doorway, grinning. 'And if you hear a fan, stay away from the window.'

DAZ

Zoe wiv me now and evryfing shoud be grate but is not. i watch her in the partmen. she lucking at fings and i can see she dont lykem. any ovver Subby i be glad, fink ah well now you see how it is but not wiv Zoe. i wish ther coud be somfing Zoe lyke but we got noffing. i always new that but it never feal so bad lyke now. i fink if Subbys'd let her back she go and i never see her again. i howld her hand and she make a littel smile but not happy.

Oh Zoe i do anifing 2 make you happy. wolk a fousan myle. slap Cal mouf.

anifing.

ZOE

So there I was, alone with the old lady. The pill was working and she was okay with me, but still and all I knew I wasn't welcome and that's a bad feeling.

I thought the stuff I'd brought might make it better so I got my anorak and emptied the pockets on to the table. She sat and watched, saying nothing. I'd hoped her face might light up or something but it didn't. When everything was on the table I said, 'This stuff's for you. I hope you can use it.' She looked at it for a minute and then she said, 'Is this all you brought?' I felt a stab of anger. Here I was trying to be friends with her, giving her stuff she'd probably never seen in her life and all she could do was criticise because I hadn't brought more. I looked at her, 'What d'you mean, all? Can you get stuff like this, even in small quantities?'

She shook her head. 'Didn't mean that, girl. This house never saw such goodies. What I mean is, where's your clothes? Shoes? The stuff you're wearing won't last forever, y'know, and you can't just go to the store and buy more like you could in Silverdale.' She nodded at the food and things. 'You better hang on to that – it'll get you strong shoes and a change of underwear, but you'd have done better to bring them along in the first place.'

She really put me down. I'd planned to offer my little store of cash, too, but she'd only tell me I was going to need it, which was true. 'Look,' I said. 'I had to leave

131

in a hurry. I had no time to plan, but I thought it'd be nice to bring along some of the stuff you can't get here, that's all.'

To my surprise she leant across the table and squeezed my arm. 'It was a nice thought, only –.' Tears glittered in the creases at the corners of her eyes. 'Can you imagine my face with lipstick? This face? And what's the use of being clean and smelling nice for a week if you've got to go back to –.'

She broke off and got up, gathering the three chipped mugs. I followed her out to the kitchen. I know it's silly, but I expected she'd run hot water into the sink, squirt in some washing-up liquid, wash the mugs and hand them over hot and steamy for me to wipe.

There was a sink. A stainless steel one, but like the elevator you only had to see it to know it hadn't been used in a long time. Its taps were dry and rusted and a foul smell rose from its drain. On a worktop beside it stood a battered plastic bucket with water in it. The water looked grey and scummy and Mrs Barraclough did the mugs in it, dipping them quickly and standing them upside down on the drainer. I looked around for something to wipe with and she said, 'Leave 'em, they'll dry.'

'Where d'you get the water?' I asked.

'Raintank on the roof.'

'But it doesn't come through your taps?'

'No. Folks'd waste it if it did. You gotta go up for it.'

'Can I get some now?'

'No. You heard Daz. You gotta stay out of sight, and anyway we've got our ration for today.'

'That?' I nodded at the bucket.

'That for washing. This to drink.' She opened a sliding door under the sink to reveal a second bucket, threequarters full. For some reason it reminded me I needed to go to the john. I mentioned it and she said

132

'Well – I was beginning to think Subbies must've found a way to do without. Second door.'

Oh, you needn't worry. I'm not going to dwell on it. If I tell you the Barracloughs have three plastic buckets in all, you've probably got the picture.

When I returned to the kitchen, she'd left it, and I was about to go back to the living room when I heard a familiar sound. I looked out the window, leaning across the sink to do it. There were high buildings all round so you couldn't see much sky, but the noise grew and I saw a fan go over, low. I ducked back, though the window was so dirty I doubt a pigeon on the sill could've seen me. As the fan's engine faded I heard a siren not far off and a minute later a copcar went by, travelling fast.

The old lady was back in her armchair. The pill must've been wearing off because she glowered at me as I came in the room.

'Hear that?' She nodded toward the street. 'They're looking for you, girl. If that boy don't hurry you're back in Silverdale and we're dead.'

I couldn't think of anything to say. I sat in the other chair and we stared at the stove, avoiding each other's eyes.

DAZ

wots the rottenest feeling?
   scairt? no
   hungry? no
   cold? no
   loanly? no
   sick? no
   ashamed ov yor movver, ashamed ov yor hoam. thats
wot.

○   □   ○

i tecka big chanse go up the school see Mister James. I
disser pointim but he like me just the same. hes teeching.
i wayt. braketyme he coms owt sez wot you doing hear
Barraclough you xpelt. i com rite owt wiv it. you in
FAIR Mister James i sez.

   he goes wite. goes shush. lucks all rownd. howd you
know that he sez. i larf. fings, i sez. fings you say fings
you do. just then a fan coms over lo and he damnear
fills his pants.

   wot you want he sez. mebbe he finks i com 2 black
male him or somfing.

want you 2 hyde some 1 i sez.

hide some 1 he sez. hoo.

girl i sez. Subby girl. name dont matter.

Subby girl he sez. i cant hyde no subby girl. thay catch me, i get kickowt Silverdale. Mister James liv in Silverdale come 2 town 5 daze a weak.

you wont get court i sez. lornoders wont luck in school cos you Subby.

thay mite he sez. thay know i'm sim pafetick.

if you sim pafetick i sez you hyde her. Mam and me get topt if you dont. i hear copcar syren, gotta get back.

okay he sez bring her after dark i do wot i can but i cant hyde her long. a day or 2 at moast. fanks Mister James i sez.

going hoam i seen abowt 6 copcars plus the fan. fan gotta speeka on it. lornorder tell frou the speeka how Subby girl missing. hare color. wot cloaths she got on. all lyke that. big reward 4 any 1 turn her in or giv informashun.

i go faster. You fink abowt gerrin topt, you go faster 2.

ZOE

We must've sat the best part of an hour, listening. It's amazing how sound travels. The guys in the fan kept moving from place to place, hovering to do their spiel about me. They got closer and closer till the tinny voice seemed to be directly over us, then moved off. I felt a little better as the noise receded, but no matter where they went we could still hear them, and of course we both realised that at this very moment somebody – one of the kids from last night – might be leading a bunch of cops here. When footfalls sounded on the stairs we tensed up and our eyes met across the cold stove, and when the outer door opened I half-rose ready to run, though I don't know where I thought I'd run to.

It was Daz. He closed the room door and leaned against it, breathing hard.

'They're everywhere,' he gasped. 'In the sky, on the ground, underground for all I know. You'd think it was a king they were looking for.'

His mother looked at him. 'Any in this building?'

He shook his head. 'Not yet. Couple of cars in the next street.' He turned to me. 'Come on – I know a place you can hide till they've gone.'

I followed him out of the room, out of the apartment and down the twilit stairs. 'Daz,' I whispered. 'Where are you taking me?'

'Basement,' he said.

We passed the doorway we came in last night and

went on down. It was totally dark and knee-deep in trash and it stank. Daz switched on a flashlight and led me toward an enormous old furnace. In the dark above it, pipes filled the ceiling space like spaghetti, but the air was cold and dank and I knew nobody had stoked *this* furnace in years. I knew what Daz had in mind too, and it crossed my mind that this wasn't exactly the most original hiding place ever devised. In fact if I was a cop, it'd be one of the first places I'd look.

I'd underestimated him. He didn't open the door and tell me to get in. The furnace stood on a brick base, very close to the wall: so close that when he shone his torch on it I noticed that whoever had limewashed the walls down here back in the good old days hadn't been able to get at this section, which was black and greasy and furred with cobwebs.

'Halfway along there,' he said, 'there's a hole in the base. It's a crawlspace, goes right in under the furnace.' He chuckled. 'I used to hide from our mam in there. I know it's not so nice, Zoe, but I want you to wait in there till I come back for you.'

He was right. It wasn't nice. I had to scrape along sideways and by the time I reached the hole my damp face was caked with cobwebs and flakes of rust and my hair was an old mop, stiff with dirt.

Under the furnace was horrible. Pitch black and horrible. I won't go on about it. I forced myself not to think about spiders and black beetles and thought about Daz as a little boy, hiding here from his mother. I wondered whether his brother Del had come here too, but that started me thinking about ghosts so I shook my head and thought about something else.

The cops came, eventually. I heard them on the stairs, then at the foot of the stairs where they paused to voice their disgust as flashlights showed the dirt they'd have to wade through in their shiny boots. I hoped it'd put them off: that their search would be perfunctory. I hoped one of them wouldn't turn out to be a Sherlock Holmes, the sort of guy who'd notice torn cobwebs and scuffmarks in the dirt. I doubted it. My hidey-hole was a good one.

They didn't find me. They spent a minute, maybe a minute and a half in the place. They looked in the furnace – I heard the door squeak – then one of them hit the boiler with something and the great hollow boom damn near creamed my brain, but that was all.

I listened as they went back up the stairs. After that it was just a matter of waiting for Daz to come. Wondering if he would, and what I'd do if he didnt? Suppose he'd been arrested, and his mother too? Suppose they never came back – what then?

I was doing a pretty good job of driving myself crazy in that dark little hole when I heard his voice.

○ □ ○

I was filthy all over, but he took me in his arms and hugged me. I felt wonderful but I knew I didn't look it and I was glad he couldn't see me. I asked him what had happened with the cops.

'Routine search, Zoe. No tipoff, so they don't know I'm involved yet, but they will. Your old man must be loaded – they're offering big peanuts for you and somebody's gonna collect before long. That's why we've got to get you out of here.'

'Yes, but where?'

'School.'

'School?'

'That's right.' He steered me toward the stairs and we climbed stealthily up the four flights to the apartment. He went first, pressing himself against walls and peeping round corners, but all the doors were shut, the stairs and landings deserted. He turned and winked at me. 'Can't beat a visit from the law for making people stay home.'

Back in the apartment I had to visit that awful bucket again. Then Daz sat me down and told me about the teacher, James. Mrs Barraclough was lying down so we had the room to ourselves. When he'd finished I said, 'Okay, so I hide in the school, but what happens to you when the cops get their tipoff – you and your mum?'

He shrugged. 'I dunno, Zoe. James said something about seeing a guy, but I didn't know what he meant.' He chuckled. 'I don't think he knew himself, he was so scairt. We'll just have to see what happens.'

I spread my hands, palms up, on my knees and looked at them. They were filthy. So were my jeans. There were cobwebs all down the front of my jumper and I felt itchy. I remembered the bucket of cold, scummy water in the kitchen and right then I'd have given anything to be standing in our gleaming shower back home. Tears filled my eyes and ran down my cheeks and I wiped at them with my fingers, knowing I was smearing dirt on my face. Daz got up and knelt by my chair and put his arms round me. He must've had a fair idea why I was crying and he didn't say anything, just knelt there, rocking me in his arms like you would a little kid.

I hadn't been a Chippy very long but I was beginning to understand why Mrs Barraclough had to have those pills.

139

O □ O

As soon as it was properly dark we set off for the school. I'd wanted to clean myself up a bit before I went but Mrs Barraclough said I'd be safer the way I was. In fact, she persuaded me to take off my jumper, which was quite new, and put on an old one of hers which was through at the elbow and far too big for me. She had me take off my wristwatch and put it in my pocket. She thought people might notice my shoes, too, but she was nowhere near my size so we decided I'd have to risk it. They were pretty messed up from the dump and anyway it was dark.

It was drizzling, too, and we didn't see many people as we trudged through the unlighted streets. The police always withdraw to the suburbs at night so we didn't expect to encounter cops and we didn't. It was almost seven when we got to the school, which was housed in a low wooden building which stood by itself on the edge of a vast, derelict site. The place in darkness but the door was open, and as we let ourselves in the teacher hurried forward.

'Anyone see you come in here, Barraclough?'

Daz shook his head. 'Don't think so, sir. This is Zoe. Zoe, this is Mister James who's gonna look after you.'

'Only for a day or so,' reminded the teacher. 'I'm taking a big risk, y'know. If they find her here they'll close the school and strip me of my status.'

Daz chuckled. 'What's the matter, sir – don't you like it here? I thought you loved us Chippy kids. Wouldn't it be great to be near us all the time?'

The teacher shuddered. 'Heaven forbid. You'd better go now, Barraclough, but don't let anyone see you,

140

and remember you've got to come up with a different arrangement for this young woman pretty soon.'

We embraced briefly and then he was gone. I followed the teacher through the lobby, across the single classroom and into a tiny washroom. In this room stood a step-ladder, and a trapdoor in the ceiling was open.

James looked at me. 'Why a child like you should want to leave Silverdale to live in a place like this I don't know. What I do know is this – that if I had my way I'd take you, by force if necessary, and restore you to your parents this very night.' He indicated the trapdoor. 'Climb through there. You'll find blankets, a flask of soup and a torch. It's the best I could manage. Use the torch only when absolutely necessary and be very quiet, especially during school hours. All right?'

I nodded and said, 'You live in Silverdale, sir?'

'I do. Why'd you ask?'

'Well – I was wondering – I mean, could you get a message to my parents, tell them I'm alive and – you know?'

He smiled sadly, shaking his head. 'Your parents are frantic with grief, Zoe. What d'you think they'd do if I showed up with a message like that? D'you think they'd say, Oh fine – when you see her again, give her our best. D'you think they'd do that?'

I shook my head and he said. 'You're right, they wouldn't. They'd call DS and say There's a guy here knows where our child is, and DS would hang me by the thumbs till I told them where you were and who'd been hiding you, and then they'd go get young Barraclough and his widowed mother and hang them.'

So that was that. He held the ladder and I climbed up. In the roofspace I found the things he'd mentioned, plus a couple of necessities he hadn't mentioned and I won't, either. And that's where I spent the next two days.

141

DAZ

thay say trubble coms in 3s rite? 6s be mor lyk it. i leeve
Zoe up the school so trubble number 1 okay for a bit.
don't get me rong – i drather hav her wiv me enityme.

nex morning 2 lornorders com nokking. thay got a
kid wiv em. i open the doar. 1 ov em sez is this the guy
and the kid sez yeah. you can see by his face he finks he
got his dirty littel pause on the peanuts alreddy. wot
guy i sez. wot you on abowt. Zoe May Askew sez the
cop. wear is she. hoo, i sez. never herd ov her i sez. this
kid seen you wiv her he sez. i luck at the kid. this kid, i
sez. this kids the biggest liar in town – say anifing 4 a
peanut. thay push me asyde, start going frou the place,
opening doars, chucking fings abowt. or mam so scairt
she crys. i'm scairt 2 cos i remember Zoe jumper wot
she swop wiv our Mam. lornorders fynd it, we ded.

thay go frou the place lyke a hurry cane but dont
find noffing. it make em reely mad. 1 ov em sez lissen –
we know she woz hear. you hiding her somwear but we
fynd her and wen we do you ded, boaf ov you.

wen thay gon i sez 2 Mam wear Zoe jumper. shes just
popt her pill and she larfs. hear, she sez, and she pulls
up her old jumper and i see Zoe jumper undaneaf. yor
a cool 1 Mam i sez. no she sez i'm a warm 1 and she
larfs again.

i dont know wear she gets em from.

Same day the lornorders com, rite? same day i'm wolking frou town finking wot 2 do abowt Zoe wen i seen Mick coming tord me. Mick dont tork 2 me no more, so i fink wen he sees me he mebbe cross the road but he dont. insted he coms up 2 me and he sez Cal onto you boy. wotcha mean i sez, finking its abowt Zoe. Pete, he sez. i dont know no Pete, i sez, but my hart jump and he seen it in my face. He larfs. You knowd him wel enuff 2 shootim, he sez. i dint shoot no 1 i sez. i got no gun. lissen he sez. Pete shot wiv Del gun. Cal knows cos Del gun always leave funny mark on shell and he fownd the shell wot kilt Pete. Then a cuppla days ago a guy sells a gun 2 Cal frend in the Diamond. Del gun, rite? Cal frend dont know this guy but Cal lucking 4 him 2 arstim hoo sholtim the gun, and if it turns owt 2 be Daz Subby-lover Barraclough, Cal gonna killim.

Mick grabs my arm, shoves his face near mine and sez i hoap it's you Barraclough you roten sod. That Pete woz a frend ov mine see. I'd kill you myself only Cal do it slower. then he larfs again and wolks of.

Mick you havent maid my day. i got lornorders plus Dred after me. All i need now is creechers from ota space and fings'll be pretty tuff.

ZOE

I don't know if you've ever spent any time in a roof-space. If you have you'll know it can get unbelievably cold at night. I had three thick blankets, but I used one folded as a mattress and the other two weren't enough to keep me from shivering most of that first night. Maybe it was fear as much as cold that caused it. I can't tell you what it's like to be hunted – you'd have to experience it but I hope you never do. Anyway I didn't get much sleep.

Daytime was worse, in a way. I woke from a doze and somebody was moving about below. I looked at my watch. It was only eight fifteen so it must be James. My legs and feet were frozen. I sat up and massaged them and it worked to some extent and then I felt hungry. I'd drunk more than half the soup last night and when I reopened the flask the rest was barely warm. I glugged it down, trying not to think about Mum's pancakes.

After breakfast it was plastic bucket by torchlight time. Don't ever try it.

The kids started arriving at eight forty-five. I don't know how many there were but they made a terrific racket. I could've boogied up and down the roof-space playing electric base and nobody'd have known I was there, but at nine on the dot it all went quiet and for the next three hours I sat like a stuffed owl, listening for sirens.

At twelve the kids erupted as school recessed for

lunch. I expected a noisy hour in which I'd be able to move about a bit and stretch my legs, but after a minute or two the whoops and hollers receded and soon the place was silent.

Then there came a knock on the trap which damn near brought on a heart attack till James's voice said, 'Okay, Zoe – it's only me.'

He'd brought me lunch – a packet of egg mayonnaise sandwiches which I demolished while he watched from his perch on the rim of the trap. I took a long drink from the can of coke he gave me, then said, 'Where did the kids go?'

He shrugged. 'Home, I guess. They're through for the day.'

'School's just mornings?'

'For them it is. Second shift starts one thirty.'

'You mean different kids?'

'Ah-ha. Older. There're not many schools out here, y'know – not nearly enough for all the kids who'd like to come. They all operate the two-shift system but the waiting lists get no shorter.' He smiled. 'I better go. Some eager pupil might arrive early and catch me.'

He look my litter and flask and went, saying he'd look in again after school. I promised myself that if I was still here tonight I'd climb down, empty my bucket and treat myself to a really good wash.

The thought kept me cheerful through afternoon school.

The second night was better. Instead of soup, James had filled the flask with coffee and there were sandwiches. There was also a hint that I might be out tomorrow, but when I tried to question him he refused to be drawn.

When darkness came I kept the promise I'd made to myself. It was harder than I'd expected because I daren't use the torch and when I opened the trap the step ladder wasn't there. Well, of course it isn't, you idiot, I told myself. He didn't know you were planning to come down, and it'd be a dead givaway if the cops decided to search the school, wouldn't it? He might as well pin up a little card with an arrow on it saying this way to the fugitive.

So what I had to do was lower myself through the trap, hang by my hands and drop. I know what you're thinking. You're thinking, how'd she do that while carrying a plastic bucket, right? Well, I didn't. I dropped empty-handed, dragged out the ladder, set it up and went back for the bucket. Easy, but of course there was a snag – I'd have to leave the ladder in place when I climbed back up, so there was no way I could hide what I was doing. The teacher would know I'd been down.

The water was cold and the one bit of soap I found refused to lather, but I really enjoyed that wash. I even washed my hair as best I could. It wasn't till I'd finished and was wet practically all over that I realised there was no towel. I had to dry myself on one of my blankets and if you think blankets make good towels you're wrong. Anyway, I managed, rubbing away till my body glowed from the friction and I felt better than I'd felt in days. I had to put on the same old dirty clothes afterwards, which was a bit of a bummer but couldn't be helped.

I even slept. Not all night, because it was cold again and I was short one blanket, but I must've zonked for

146

some hours because the night seemed to go in a flash, and as things turned out it was as well I got that rest, because it was going to be a busy day.

To say the least.

DAZ

I'm downtown nex day scoring tucker wen I seen this guy i rekernise. He sees me 2 and coms over. Hear he sez, wots rong wiv that gun you solt me?

Noffing i sez, why?

2 guys grab me lars nite in the club, he sez. Arst hoo solt it me.

Wos 1 of em a littel guy wiv spex?

yea thats rite, and the ovver wos a big 1 wiv mussels.

Did you tel em?

Coudnt coud i – dont know yor name. Tolt em wot you luck lyke thogh.

Fanks.

Yea, well – they luck lyke thay mean biznis, know wot i mean?

I knew wot he ment alrite. i dint hang abowt. Set of hoam fast as i coud. Lornorders evrywear plus Cal gang lucking 4 me. O Zoe my lov, if i dont maykit wotl hapen 2 you?

Gotta maykit.

ZOE

My sleep ended with a bang at eight fifteen as James came storming up the ladder and flung back the trap. In my fuddled state I thought it was DS and was trying to crawl into a corner when he barked, 'You were out last night, weren't you?'

'Not out sir,' I said, returning to my blankets. 'I went down for a wash, and to empty the bucket.'

'You should have asked me. I'd have emptied the damned bucket. Meant to anyway and forgot. I'd have brought soap and water too, if you'd mentioned it. I suppose you showed a light?'

Boy, was he mad! 'Of course not,' I said. 'I'm not stupid.'

'No? Then why are you here, living like a hunted animal and putting other people's lives at risk when you could have stayed home and lived in comfort the rest of your life?'

I looked at him. 'You live in Silverdale too. Why do you come here? You could teach in Silverdale for more money and less hassle, but you don't.'

'No, I don't.' He sighed. 'Listen, Zoe. I'm sorry I blew up just now, but I don't think you fully realise what's at stake here. You came out of Silverdale because you didn't want to move to Peacehaven with your folks. You wanted to stay because you believe yourself to be in love with Darren Barraclough, and for that you were prepared to put his life and that of his mother in

149

jeopardy. But there's more at risk even than that. You've heard of an organization known as FAIR?'

I nodded. 'Yes, and you're a member. Daz told me. And by the way I don't just believe myself in love with him – I am.'

'All right. So you know about FAIR, and you know I'm a member. Do you know any other members?'

'No.'

'You sure about that?'

'Sure I'm sure.' He was starting to sound like Pohlman.

'What about your friend's father, Wentworth?'

'Oh – oh yeah. I forgot about him.' I hadn't. I just thought it'd be better not to mention him.

'And the lady who wrote this – did you forget her too?' He pulled a crumpled envelope from his pocket and handed it to me. I looked at it. 'There's nothing on this. No writing at all.'

'Open it.'

'Why – what is it?'

'Open it, Zoe.'

I poked my finger under the flap, ripped it across and drew out a flimsy folded sheet which I opened and smoothed out in my lap. It was covered with tiny, cramped writing which looked familiar. I held it up so that light from the trap fell on it and looked at the signature.

Grandma, it said.

I looked at James. 'You saw my grandmother? She gave you this?'

'Certainly. Your defection has caused problems for us, Zoe. It has stirred up the authorities. Made them nervous. It's difficult for an organisation such as ours to operate in such a climate. It's particularly unfortunate that it comes hard on the heels of the Wentworth expulsion which rocked our Silverdale unit to its foundations. It was necessary to discuss your case – to try to find a way of defusing the situation before it gets completely out of hand. That's why your grandmother and I met last night.'

'Are you saying my Grandma's involved with FAIR?'

'Your grandmother *is* FAIR in Silverdale, Zoe. She founded the unit and ran it virtually single-handed for twenty years, till she decided she was too old and Wentworth took over. Think about it, Zoe – twenty years with a price on her head. Now Wentworth's out and she's back up the sharp end at the age of one hundred and four. Anyway there was this meeting and we think we have a solution. It's not perfect, but it's a lot better than your present predicament.'

'What is it?' I asked the question in a vacant sort of way – my mind was struggling to cope with the idea of Grandma as local head of an illegal organisation. I kept picturing her sweet old face on a wanted poster.

'You're to go to the Wentworth place. You leave tonight. The Barracloughs too, if you can persuade them. If you can't, you must go alone.'

'The Wentworth place? But I don't even know where it is.'

'Your grandmother does.' He nodded at the letter. 'It's all in there.'

'Do the Wentworths know about this?'

'Naturally.'

'But how – I mean, Tabby told me the place was miles away. How'd you get in touch?'

'You don't want to know that, Zoe. If you don't make it – if DS get you, then the less you know the better. Read the letter, memorise your grandma's directions and I'll destroy it when I come after school.'

He left some food and went away. I was down. I mean really depressed. In fact I guess you could say I hated myself because he made me see what I'd done. All those people including my own grandmother in danger of their lives because of me. I didn't touch the food – I had no appetite. I sat in the dark, thinking about Grandma and my parents and what it'd be like to see Tabby again. I thought about being caught by DS, too, and wondered what Daz was doing right now. After a while I switched on the torch and read Grandma's letter.

It seemed Wentworth had built his refuge in a place Grandma knew quite well – a much visited beauty spot of sixty, seventy years ago, about thirty miles east of the city. Clanton Rocks, it was called in those days. She'd written detailed instructions about how to get there, and there was a sketch map done from memory. She warned that of course things would've changed a lot in the meantime, told me to travel at night if possible and wished me luck. At the end she'd put

'We are members one of another.'

I guess that's a quote but I didn't get it at the time. I cried a bit because these were probably the last words of hers I'd ever have. Then I thought about what a tough little woman she must be to have done all she'd done, and I dried my eyes. Her blood was in my veins, wasn't it? There's a time to cry and a time to be tough, and now it was time to be tough.

When James came again, I'd be ready.

○　□　○

It was just after three when the cops arrived. I heard a siren but I'd been hearing them for two days, coming closer and closer, then fading as the cars went by.

This one didn't. Its wail swelled till it was like the car was right there in the roof-space, then it cut out abruptly and I heard doors – car doors and school doors, mixed up with voices and footsteps and the sounds excited kids make. Chairs squealed on the plank floor and I pictured cops in the schoolroom, opening, probing, overturning. Terror held me rigid. Within seconds they'd ransacked the classroom and were directly beneath me. I heard the teacher's voice raised in protest, and another I thought I'd heard before. There was some banging and cursing and milling around, and then somebody said, 'Well – she's gotta be here somewhere,' and it was Pohlman.

I heard them go back to the classroom but I knew they weren't leaving. No way. Not after what Pohlman just said. He'd obviously had a tipoff and I knew what he'd do. He'd post somebody outside in case I tried to run, and then he'd lead a far more thorough search. They'd start with the lobby and work their way through the building and nothing – not even the smallest spider – would escape their notice. And when they got to the washroom again Pohlman would see the trap, and smile.

I had to do something. I couldn't just sit shivering like a trapped animal, waiting till they came for me. Because it wasn't just me, was it? It was Grandma and Daz and Mr James and all the others. I might not die if they caught me but others would. Who knows how many in the end? I must take control of my fear and get myself out of this.

153

In total darkness I crawled, feeling my way to the trap. I hooked my fingers under its rim and raised it ever so slightly. The washroom door was open. I listened. In the schoolroom, kids were talking in subdued tones. Adult voices farther off told me I'd been right – they were searching the lobby, and it wouldn't take long. Then they'd start on the classroom, but would they search it while it was full of kids? I didn't think so, and this gave me an idea. It wasn't a brilliant idea. In fact it was probably a stupid idea which would only get me caught a few minutes sooner than if I stayed where I was, but it was the only thing I could think of so it would have to do.

I eased the trap down gently. Then, risking torchlight for the sake of speed I scooped up blankets, flask and bucket and, bent double, scurried into a far corner where I stood the bucket upside down with the flask inside. The blankets I carried to another corner, pushing them down between joists. Like all roof spaces, this one had its share of accumulated bits and pieces and I hoped the cops wouldn't notice the stuff I'd used. This done, I returned to the trap, doused the light and stuck the torch in the band of my jeans.

I raised the trap a little. The washroom was unoccupied. In the classroom a man was yelling at the kids. 'Come on, c'm on – outside. Let's go now.' It was what I'd expected. I raised the trap halfway and eased myself through, supporting the door with my shoulders, the back of my head and finally on my knuckles. I couldn't prevent the slight bang as it fell into position when I dropped, but the sound was masked by the racket the kids were making as they clattered through scattered chairs and milled around the door.

I breathed a prayer and walked out into the classroom. At the far end a cop stood, fists on hips, watching the push and shove. He wasn't looking my way and I was able to attach myself to the rear of the boisterous scrum. The kids were too busy giving the cops a hard time to notice the new pupil, and I kept my head down as we pushed toward the door.

Pohlman was my problem now. In my present filthy state I can't have looked much different from the kids around me, but the lieutenant and I had met. If we came face to face in the lobby it would all be over. I realised that if I was last out or nearly last, I'd be conspicuous. I needed to pass through the lobby in the middle of a surge of kids. I began shoving with my shoulder, worming my way through impossible gaps as I fought my way forward. I got a couple of elbows in the ribs but nobody moaned. Anything that made the cops' job harder was part of the fun.

It wasn't long until the big moment arrived. Jammed momentarily in the creaking doorframe, we exploded into the lobby and were propelled forward on to the backs of those who battled to pass the outer door. I had a glimpse of Pohlman, white with anger, pressed against the wall. He'd probably stationed himself there with the idea of scanning the kids' faces as they passed, but it hadn't worked out that way.

Around the outer door the procedure was repeated. Slowly forward, shoving and being shoved; a brief, asphyxiating hesitation during which I saw, between the heads of those in front, James looking strained with his pupil register tucked under his arm, then explosive release into air and space.

The instant I cleared the doorway I doubled back through hurtling bodies and ran, bent over like in the roof space only faster, to the corner and away along the side of the building. Every moment I expected to hear the command 'halt', but I made it to the next corner and swung round it unchallenged. I was now outside the washroom, with the building between me and everybody else and nothing but derelict land behind. I glanced around. There was nobody in sight, and as long as I stayed close to the wall I couldn't be seen from the washroom window.

I breathed in deeply, praying that Pohlman wouldn't decide to walk round the outside of the school. At the far end I heard James calling the roll, kids' voices going sir, sir, sir. I knew the instant Pohlman spotted the trap because he cried out and I heard the drag of the step ladder across the floor, the slam of the trap. As I listened, hardly daring to believe I'd given them the slip, my eyes scanned the terrain. About fifty yards away I saw a small heap of broken bricks. If the worst came to the worst – if they came round this way – that's where I'd go.

I didn't have to. They slammed around inside for a while, snarling and kicking things, then gave up. Pohlman came out and yelled at James, who wouldn't be too worried about that, but would be wondering how in blue blazes he'd got away with it and what the heck had become of me. When Pohlman was through shouting they got in the car and drove off, and after giving them a minute to get clear I walked away, eating Grandma's letter as I went.

DAZ

Cal got our pad staked owt. I seenem frou the windo soonas I got hoam. 2 guys. 1 on the corner smoaking 1 ded opozit doing noffing. Mustav seen me com hoam, told Cal. Anityme now Cal orders com and I know wot. Go in and killim thats wot.

Gotta hyde. Me and Mam. I know wear. Mam I sez. DRED coming 4 me I gotta hyde. You 2 I sez cos I know that Cal. He cant find me, top you insted no hezzy tayshon. Mam scairt. Tekka pill Mam I sez. She tekka pill, I luck owt the windo seen the 2 guys coming, pockets fat wiv guns. Com on Mam i sez. no she sez. shex her hed. i vad enuff our Daz. cant take no more. leev me hear she sez. i got my pills. you go son an god bless.

i dont wanta leaver but no tyme 2 arg you. i hit them baysmen steps as Cal guys bang frou the doar. they gon up the partmen firs or i never maykit but I got under that furniss. I dint forgoten Zoe but cant get up the school no way til Cal guys gon.

In the dark waiting I fink ov Zoe in the dark waiting and Mams god bless and i cry a littel bit. evry 1 cry somtyme even you.

157

ZOE

Three thirty-five. What I thought I'd do was find a derelict building to hide in till it got dark, then head for Daz's place. Thanks to me, the city was getting a bit too hot for Daz, and I was pretty confident he'd want to go with me to the Wentworth place. I wasn't sure about his mother, though, and I wondered whether he'd leave her if she refused to budge.

I could see a line of gutted houses about half a mile away, and I was heading toward them when I saw a sheet of paper on the ground in front of me. I noticed it because it looked clean and new and because it had my face on it.

I picked it up. It was a sort of handbill. Across the top in big black print was the word **KIDNAP**. Under the picture it said **HAVE YOU SEEN THIS GIRL?** and went on to mention a substantial reward. All you had to do was find a police officer and give your information. I screwed it up and shoved it in my pocket, but when I glanced around to see if anyone had noticed I saw the whole area littered with them. The cops must've flown over in fans, chucking the things out by the handful. It was just what I needed, my picture all over the city.

I started to walk faster, keeping my head down. I couldn't actually see anybody but the bills had thrown a scare into me and I was glad when I reached the first of the old houses.

I piled four bricks in a corner and sat on them. I saw a cat and a bird or two but no people. Toward dusk it began to drizzle. The house had no roof. My anorak was supposed to be showerproof but my shoulders were soon wet and so were my knees. By the time it was properly dark I was shivering. I got up and walked toward the city. My jeans clung to my legs and my anorak pockets were wet inside. I comforted myself with the thought that I must look just like a Chippy. I certainly felt like one.

It was still raining and there were few people to be seen as I approached the dilapidated block Daz called home. Nevertheless, I didn't go straight up to the door, but stood for a minute or two in the doorway of an abandoned shop, watching and listening. All seemed quiet. No children were playing in the lobby. I shifted my gaze to the damp-scarred face of the building till it found the right window. No light showed there, but this was not unusual. The electricity supply was sporadic because fuel to run the generator was hard to come by, and unreliable because the generator itself was ancient. An hour's uninterrupted current was an event, a full evening of TV virtually unknown. Candles burned in some of the windows but candles, too, were in short supply.

I crossed the road and walked into the dark lobby. It was deserted. The dead elevator wore a shroud of shadow. The stench was familiar now. I took the stairs.

The door of the apartment stood open. I took one step into the hallway and stopped.

'Daz?' No answer.

'Mrs Barraclough?' Silence. The place had an empty feel to it, yet I couldn't believe neither occupant was in. Daz often went out after dark, I knew that, but his mother didn't. Ever. she told me. So she had to be here, unless –.

I heard a small sound behind me but before I could react an arm was thrown round my waist, a hand clamped my mouth and a soft voice murmured in my ear. 'No noise, now. No noise at all, or the world's total of Subbies will fall by one.'

He wasn't a big guy. No taller than me, in fact, but his grip was good. I struggled for a while and lashed out backwards with my foot, but it was no use. He turned me, pushed me back to the stairs and we hobbled down, awkwardly, his mouth in my hair saying, 'Down we go. There's a good girl, now. All the way down.'

He shoved and wrestled me down to the basement where I saw two men, one with a torch and one with a gun. They were near the old furnace. The little guy pushed me toward them. The one with the torch shone it in my eyes.

'Who's this, Cal?'

Cal! So I'm at Cal's mercy now. The merciless Cal.

'This?' Cal chuckled. 'Why, this is nothing less than the answer to all our recent prayers, Mick my boy.' He faced the furnace and called, 'Hey, Mister Barraclough. Here's a friend wants to see you.' He removed his hand from over my mouth, grabbed my ear and gave it a twist that damn near tore it off. I screamed.

'Zoe?' As Daz called out I saw it all. DRED had come for him and he'd taken refuge where he'd always taken it – in the crawlspace under the furnace. They'd found him somehow, but short of dismantling the base brick by brick, there was no way they could've got him out of there. No way, that is, till I came along.

Cal released me and I considered making a run for it. If I got away, maybe Daz could hold out till morning when the police would resume their search for me and Cal would be forced to leave. He must've read my mind or something, because he smiled coldly and murmured, 'Don't even think about it. Smithy here's a crack shot.

You'd be dead before you hit the floor.' He turned. 'Darren, you're keeping the lady waiting. Where's your manners, lad?'

'If I come out,' said Daz, 'Will you let her go?'

'You have my word, and you know I'm a man of my word.'

'What'll you do to him?' I asked, though I guess I knew the answer.

He looked at me. 'Do to him? Why I'm going to kill him of course. What else?'

'Daz,' I cried, 'Don't come out. They'll kill you if you do.'

'And we'll kill her if you don't,' countered Cal, 'And we'll get you anyway, in the end.'

I'm no heroine. D'you know what a heroine would've done right then? A heroine in a book? She'd have made a dash for it, forced 'em to kill her so they had nothing to bargain with. It occurred to me, but I didn't do it. Couldn't. Maybe I don't love Daz enough. I don't know. Anyway, I hope you're never faced with a choice like that. You think about it afterwards and it's heavy. It screws you up.

Daz was coming out. I could hear him scraping the wall, shuffling sideways in the narrow space. Coming out to die. The guy with the torch, Mick, shone it in his face as he emerged. Daz lifted a hand to shield his eyes, looking for Cal.

'Okay, you got me. Let her go.'

Cal smiled. 'All in good time, lad. We don't want her fetching the law before we're through here, now do we?'

Daz squinted at him. 'How long does it take to kill a guy? You'll be through before she's up the stairs.'

Mick sniggered and Cal said, 'Oh no, lad. You don't understand. What we have here is a breakdown of understanding. Killing can be pretty quick, that's true, but it can also be – how shall I put it – dragged out.'

161

He gazed into Daz's eyes. 'Take Pete now. You remember Pete of course – my good friend Pete, whom you shot in the back? Yes, of course you do. Now Pete's death was one of the quick ones. In fact you could say he never knew what hit him. You on the other hand, will know exactly what hits you. We'll begin, I think, with a kneecap. Young Zoe here can watch.' He turned to me, 'Tell me, have you ever seen a kneecap blown off? Have you heard the noise the victim makes? No?' He shook his head, sadly. 'Terrible, it is. I don't even like to think about it.' As he spoke, he drew a revolver from the pocket of his raincoat. He gestured to the two men. 'Bring him over here and keep a good hold of him.' He leered at Daz. 'This is going to hurt you a lot more than it'll hurt me.' He stooped, thrusting the gun into the crook of Daz's knee. I cringed and turned my face away as the shot rang out.

The shot, and the agonised scream which followed it echoed deafeningly through the basement. Sick with horror, yet driven by a compulsion I was powerless to resist I turned. Daz, supported by Mick and Smithy, was still on his feet. Cal was kneeling on the floor with his arms wrapped round his stomach, screaming. His broken glasses lay in a crimson splotch on the floor. As I gaped, the two men let go of Daz and turned toward the stairs. I turned, too. Pohlman was crouching on the bottom step with a smoking gun in his fist. Smithy was raising his own weapon when Pohlman fired again. The gunman spun round and crumpled, his pistol skittering away across the cement. Mick, seeing Pohlman momentarily distracted, doused his torch and made a dash for it, knocking the policeman sideways and leaping on to the stairs. There was a shot, a cry and a metallic clatter. A light which had been shining from somewhere behind Pohlman went out and the basement was plunged into blackness.

A grip clamped my arm, Daz yelled, 'Come on!' and I was dragged, totally blind, across the floor. I don't know how he knew where to go, but almost at once I tripped on the first step and then we were climbing. There was a heck of a racket – shouting, shooting, some sort of motor. Anyway, there we were, going up into blackness and then I saw light – a glimmer and some flashes and we were up in the lobby and somebody had a spotlight on it so I couldn't see much more than in the dark.

I'm not sure, but I think we were shot at as we burst out on the street. Who shot at us I don't know – it might've been DRED, or the cops, or both. Or they might've been shooting at each other and we got in the way. Anyway, DRED was there in strength to engage the cops in a fire-fight, and that's what saved us. We ran through the flash and rattle of small arms fire and everybody was too busy keeping their heads down to worry about us. DS had a fan on the roof of the block and as we set off along the street it came swooping down, chasing us with its spotlamp, but when it slowed to keep pace with us it became a soft target for DRED, whose concentrated fire forced it to climb away. We ran on, gasping and sobbing, and when we stopped there was darkness all around and the fight was far behind.

We rested briefly to catch our breath and to marvel at our escape. I told Daz about the letter and what had happened at school. Daz hugged me and said I was a hero and I said no, he and his mother were the brave ones, and then suddenly we both burst into tears, which never happens to heroes in the movies.

We weren't safe yet, of course, and so once we'd got our breath back and dried our eyes and decided which way was west we moved on quickly, intent on putting as much distance as possible between ourselves and the city by dawn.

I was hungry, which isn't surprising when you remember I hadn't eaten anything all day unless you're going to count Grandma's letter, but I was too happy to care. We'd almost died, but here we were alive. Instead of the end we were moving toward the beginning of something. I knew we were. I felt it getting closer.

I could feel it getting closer.

DAZ 4 ZOE

There's this hill, right? Pinkney Hill, a few miles west of the city. It's a long climb, but quicker than going round, and beside there're woods on the far slope where we knew we'd be safe through the day. It was still dark when we started up, but dawn was breaking as we reached the top.

Well, we stood for a minute looking back, and though the sky was lightening in that direction the plain was still in shadow. There was Rawhampton and there was Silverdale, and as we watched the bouncers switched off the spot lamps and then it was impossible to tell where the city ended and the suburb began.

Glossary: reading the text

This glossary does not attempt to explain Daz's dialect and slang, but leaves the reader to explore its humour and variety. One tip: read Daz's words just as they are written!

The questions printed below in boxes are to help the reader think back over what has happened in the story so far.

Pages 1–28

6 **I.D.** identity cards.

7 **peanuts** the Chippy word for cash.

12 **snaggle** broken.

17 **dilapidated** falling to pieces.

18 **DJ** disc jockey.

19 **nauseating** sick making.

lobotomiser the name of the drink suggests it will cut into the nerves of the brain.

25 **indifference** lack of interest.

1 Why do you think the author begins *DAZ 4 ZOE* with 'A True Story'? What is he saying to his readers in the closing lines?

2 What details about Daz's family and 'Chippy' lifestyle are given in these opening pages?

3 In contrast, what picture do we have of Zoe's 'Subby' lifestyle in the early chapters?

4 What is the *mixture* of emotions felt by Zoe during her night out to visit the Blue Moon club?

5 How far into the future is the novel set? Give a date.

Pages 29–74

30 *suburbanite*   a 'Subby' – someone who lives in the suburbs.

fraternise   mix with as a friend.

33 *stumped*   puzzled, lost for words.

mooned   idled.

38 *visiting with*   seeing.

41 *Franchise*   a right or privilege.

anomaly   something not in order, irregular.

52 *contradicts*   argues with.

53 *defaced*   spoiled, written across.

54 *repentance*   saying sorry, feeling regret.

devastation   mess, destruction.

66 *perimeter*   boundary.

68 *receded*   died away.

70 *ecstatic*   wonderful.

73 *radiance*   brightness.

74 *tenderhooks*   tension, suspense.

remote surveillance watching from a distance, with the aid of technical equipment.

ostracize ignore, exclude.

---

1 Why does Zoe particularly value Grandma as a listener to her problems?

2 After Daz and Zoe have met, how do their relationships with their parents and teachers change?

3 Why does Zoe write the word 'Brainwashing' across the lines for Miss Moncrieff? When might you use this word?

4 Why does Zoe retell the story of Galileo (pages 54–5)? How does it help her to deal with Miss Moncrieff and her parents?

5 How does Robert Swindells bring out both the humour and the desperation of Daz's trip through the tunnel? Look carefully at the language.

Pages 75–106

81 **intercepted** seized.

imposition punishment.

83 **expansive** open, friendly.

84 **interrogation** close questioning.

85 **proscribed** banned.

89 **schlepped** dragged.

bogus false.

93 **desolation** hopelessness, depression.

psychological in the mind.

94 **obsessive** haunted, constantly thinking about someone.

humiliated me hurt my pride.

95 *retard*   backward person.

janitor   caretaker.

97 *hunkered down*   sat on my haunches.

affirmation   agreement.

00 *apprehension*   worry, fear.

01 *recoiled*   drew back.

---

1   What picture do you form of Domestic Security (DS)? Why does Lieutenant Pohlman find Zoe difficult to deal with?

2   Why does Daz have no time for FAIR (page 92)? Contrast his view of the organisation with the views Zoe's father holds about FAIR.

3   Why is the school so abrupt with Zoe when she wants to find out what has happened to Tabby?

4   What are the reasons why both Zoe's and Tabby's parents want to move from Silverdale? Are they the same or different?

5   'Later, I was to find out she'd been brooding about something far more important than my problem' (page 106). What do you guess Grandma is thinking about at this point?

Pages 107–133

09 *contemplate*   think carefully about.

foodstamps and clothing vouchers   coupons to be used instead of money.

13 *conspicuous*   easily seen.

14 *commodity*   possession.

116 *tenuous*   flimsy.

strollers   pushchairs.

118 *enormity*   frightening scale.

119 *materialised*   appeared.

dejected gait   miserable way of moving.

121 *scornfully*   with contempt.

122 *panorama*   wide view.

shanties   crude huts.

listless   with no energy.

124 *antiseptic*   clean and pure.

125 *transparent*   obvious.

126 *lustreless*   dull, without any sparkle.

127 *harbour*   shelter.

compromised   agreed.

133 *glowered*   stared angrily.

---

1   As Zoe is deciding to leave home, what aspects of life there does she think she'll miss most?

2   What is your reaction to Daz's shooting of Pete (page 111)? Is revenge sweet?

3   'I found myself overwhelmed by a combination of emotions, the strongest of which were regret, sheer disbelief and rising panic' (page 118). Analyse what Zoe means here.

4   What are Mrs Barraclough's reactions to Zoe's leaving Silverdale and arriving in Rawhampton? Do you find her a sympathetic character?

Pages 134–165

36 *spiel*   broadcast.

38 *perfunctory*   careless.

40 *encounter*   meet.

44 *recessed*   took a break.

51 *defection*   changing sides.

defusing   playing down.

predicament   situation.

53 *ransacked*   searched very thoroughly.

54 *subdued*   quiet.

55 *boisterous*   noisy.

asphyxiating   suffocating.

59 *sporadic*   going on and off.

60 *dismantling*   taking apart.

62 *compulsion*   inner force.

63 *skittering*   skimming.

doused   put out.

1   Page 134: why does Daz dwell on these particular questions and answers at this point? Can you identify with his answers?

2   Why does Mr James agree to help Daz and Zoe? What does he think of her leaving Silverdale?

3   What is Zoe's reaction to the news that her Grandma *is* FAIR in Silverdale (page 151)? Why did Grandma write the words: 'We are members one of another'?

4   Why does the author end page 157 with the words: 'i cry a littel bit. evry 1 cry somtyme even you'?

5   '... and then it was impossible to tell where the city ended and the suburb began' (page 165). What is intended by the author in finishing the novel with these words?

6   As you finish reading **DAZ 4 ZOE**, would you change your first guess as to when the novel is set?

Study programme

Starters

1. Who said or thought the following? And at what point in the novel?

   - *A lobotomiser. It's coke with rum and a couple of other ingredients. Try one?*

   - *Not easy, our mam. Not easy.*

   - *You rush inter fings, end up ded. Speshly in tunnels.*

   - *The guard opened fire but the man made off into the darkness. An exhaustive search failed to find him.*

   - *Don't some of the kids call you names? One name in particular? Don't they call you Chippy-lover?*

   - *Your parents have decided to move, and since you are not yet old enough to look after yourself you have no choice but to go with them.*

   - *I mentioned a smell before – the one that was strong in some places and faint in others.*

   - *What I do know is this – that if I had my way I'd take you, by force if necessary, and restore you to your parents this very night.*

2. Write down five 'open' questions about events in the story which you can ask someone else who has just read the book. For example:

   - Why didn't Grandma do more to help Zoe?

   - How would you have reacted to Lieutenant Pohlman's questioning?

3. Make a sketch of one striking scene from the novel.

4. Write down in no more than 100 words a short piece about **DAZ 4 ZOE** that could be placed in a magazine to encourage other students to read the book.

5. Note down three alternative titles for **DAZ 4 ZOE**.

6. Put together a collage of cuttings and photos (from magazines and newspaper) of a scene, incident or idea from the novel.

7. What year is the novel set in? Give reasons for your answer.

Plot

1. Draw a time-line on which you place the main events of the novel. Begin with page 10: 'It was a Friday'.

   This task will require a skim reread of the book. Use your Reading Log if you have kept one. You could present your work as a wall display.

2. What sort of a picture do you have of the areas where Daz and Zoe live?

   Draw a plan of the two different districts, using information from the book. Label the plan with boxes in which you note 'key moments' in the narrative.

3. Put yourself in the shoes of a film director. S/he wants to prepare for a film of **DAZ 4 ZOE** and needs a series of images for planning. Create about a dozen storyboards which capture what for you are the highlights of the novel.

4 Are there any points in the novel where you wished the author had filled in more detail or concentrated more on a particular incident?

Write two additional short chapters to slot into **DAZ 4 ZOE**. Write one from Zoe's and one from Daz's viewpoint. Plan carefully when writing in the same style as Daz!

5 You are a Subby journalist visiting Rawhampton. You have been asked by the editor of a teenage magazine to file a story: 'A day in the Life of a Chippy'. Write your article, complete with headline and sub-headings; add clip-art or similar if you present word-processed copy.

6 Robert Swindells has said that plot is more important to him than character because as a child reader he was always more interested in the situation than the characters. Is this true in **DAZ 4 ZOE**? Prepare some notes on the subject. With a partner, debate your views, making sure you use examples from the book to support what you say.

Characters

Zoe

1 What do you know about Zoe as a person? Look through the book and note down:

- what she says about herself
- what others say about her
- any actions and reactions which show her personality

Discuss and compare your notes with a partner. Now write them up as a Character Study of Zoe.

Daz

2 What sort of a person is Daz? Note down:

- what he says about himself
- what others say about him
- behaviour which reveals his personality

Compare your notes with a partner and then write them up as a Character Study of Daz.

3 'wots the rottenest feeling?'

Look again at Daz's words on page 134. Write a series of short diary entries in which Daz thinks about what his family life has become. Try to capture his depressed mood.

Grandma

4 'Gran says she remembers the city that way but it's hard to imagine.' Reread the second paragraph on page 15.

Write a short biography of Grandma. Trace how life changed during her many years in Rawhampton. Try to track the gradual breakdown of city life – how did it come about, step-by-step? Include details of how she came to be a member of FAIR.

5 The novel is mainly about Daz and Zoe. But it also describes their conflicts with their parents.

Imagine Mr and Mrs Askew meeting up with Mrs Barraclough after Daz and Zoe have run away. Improvise a scene between the three parents in which they:

- talk about their own lifestyle
- talk about their children
- try to explain to each other what has has happened, how and why

6 Working in groups, 'hotseat' each of the main characters, asking them to explain why they acted the way they did at different moments in the book.

7 It is often said that an author 'loads the dice' for and against his characters and what they stand for. Discuss in a group who you think Robert Swindells seems to be 'for' or 'against'. Look closely at the text to support your view with quotations.

8   *I'm no heroine. D'you know what a heroine would've done right then? A heroine in a book?*

page 161

   and then suddenly we both burst into tears, which never happens to heroes in the movies.

page 164

In what ways is the novel a classic story of heroes and heroines? What are your images of movie heroes? Talk about your ideas in groups and then write up your conclusions.

Language and style

1 In an interview, Robert Swindells noted: 'I think writing in the first person makes the story more immediate because readers think it is happening to them. It has its drawbacks, in that you have only one point of view; the "I" in your book can't know what's happening elsewhere. You need to use devices such as being told by another character. In **Stone Cold**, **DAZ 4 ZOE** and **Follow a Shadow** I got over the problem with two first-person narrators.'

- Think about other books you've read. Are they told in the first or third person? Make a list of the advantages and disadvantages as you see them.
- What is your view on the use of the double narrator in **DAZ**

4 ZOE? Where do you think it is effective? List some examples in the book where we hear about the same event from two different angles. One example would be to compare pages 29 and 36 when Daz and Zoe first start thinking about each other.

2 The author recalls that when he was a child he liked books with short chapters that made you want to 'read on'.

In a group, discuss how he employs short chapters in this novel. Look closely at how each chapter ends. Note down a selection of the phrases and sentences that are used.

3 Although the book is often gloomy and violent, there is a lot of humour in the writing. Write down a selection of witty lines. For example:

- *i go faster. You fink abowt gerrin topt, you go faster 2.*

  page 135

- *Hang in there, Galileo. Way to go, man!*

  page 55

4 One technique of writing that the author uses quite often is to invite the reader *into* the novel to share what a character is thinking or feeling – to climb inside a character's skin. For example:

> *If you love someone – really love them, and if you can imagine how it'd feel to leave them with a very strong chance you'd never meet again – ever – then you've got it. And if you don't, and can't, it's no use my trying to put it into words.*

  pages 92–3

Working with a partner, write down other examples of this technique.

5 Daz says on page 65: 'no magic in my riting so i stop now'. And yet his style has the quality of being chatty, funny and easy to read once you get used to it.

Try writing a paragraph from a Zoe chapter in Daz's style. Then recast a short Daz chapter in standard English. Compare the versions with a partner. What is lost or gained in the 'translations'?

6 Daz has his own Chippy dialect which includes its own vocabulary. Make a list of these words with their standard English equivalent. To get you started:

fan	helicopter
peanuts	cash
lornorders	police

7 Daz also has his own spelling system. What are your thoughts on it? Working with a partner, make a list of how he spells some words alongside their standard English equivalent:

rite	right
larfs	laughs
biznis	business
whassamarra?	what's the matter?

8 People have been calling for simpler spelling of English words since at least the sixteenth century.

The playwright George Bernard Shaw (1856–1950) devised a new alphabet and observed that the word 'fish' could reasonably be spelled 'ghoti' – 'gh' as in cough, 'o' as in women, 'ti' as in nation. Recently the Simplified Spelling Society in Britain suggested we cut all unnecessary letters from words: e.g. the 'g' in gnaw or the 'b' in debt.

What are the main arguments for and against changing the spelling of English? Look at how the great English writers Geoffrey Chaucer and William Shakespeare wrote the language? How has it changed over the centuries? How will it go on changing as a world language – perhaps because of the Internet and speed of communications? Research and prepare some notes. In groups, stage a debate on the subject.

Themes and ideas

1 Discuss the following with a partner. Which statements best sum up for you the ideas in the novel? *DAZ 4 ZOE* is about:

- teenage rebellion
- conflicting generations
- street gangs
- a divided society
- a future world

- teenage love
- gang warfare
- the breakdown of law and order
- class differences
- community responsibilities

Are there any other ideas you would add?

Now write an essay titled 'Themes and Ideas in *DAZ 4 ZOE*'.

2 Think about the two contrasting groups in the novel: Chippies and Subbies. Write down a list of headings:

- language
- values
- attitudes
- homes
- work and leisure

Place under each of these headings a short sentence of your own – and/or a quotation from the text – which describes the Chippy and Subby lifestyles. These could be mounted – with illustrations – for a wall display.

In groups, discuss whether this view of a future world is believable. Does Robert Swindells stereotype his characters to make a point?

3 Role-play a chat between Daz and Zoe ten years later, thinking back on their teenage years. What do they remember? What is the situation in Silverdale and Rawhampton now?

4 In an interview about his work, the author commented:

> I believe young people enjoy being worried and frightened while reading – providing it all comes out okay in the end! If a situation doesn't disturb anybody it will probably continue. I don't pussyfoot around – I go straight for the jugular.

Write a letter to the author in which you comment on the content, style and levels of violence in **DAZ 4 ZOE**.

5 In the same interview, the author goes on to say:

> a novel with no viewpoint – no politics in the widest sense – will have very little of anything else in it either. My fiction for teenagers is a form of propaganda.

Look up the meaning of the word 'propaganda'. Think about other novels you've read which have a strong viewpoint in them. With particular reference to **DAZ 4 ZOE**, stage a group debate on the subject 'The duty of the writer is to disturb a reader'.

6 In 1995 the Rowntree Foundation published some worrying statistics. The figures showed that, between 1985 and 1995, the top 10 per cent of those in work had increased their earnings by 61 per cent. In the same period, the bottom 10 per cent had dropped in their earnings by 17 per cent.

Write down some notes on the ways in which 'the rich get richer while the poor get poorer'. Now discuss in groups ways in which society might try to stop the gap widening. Think about the final lines of the novel's opening chapter.

7 At the end of his 'Writer on writing' piece, Robert Swindells says: 'I leave it to my reader to decide whether ... the society my book portrays is the sort of thing we ought to be aiming at'.

Write a letter to your local newspaper which responds to those words. You could begin:

> Dear Editor,
> I have just finished reading a powerful novel called **DAZ 4 ZOE**. It describes a world set not too far into the future when our cities are divided into 'rich' and 'poor' zones. When I look around in my own neighbourhood I can see some worrying signs now that are dividing our own local community ...

In your letter, try to bring to the reader's attention signs in society of change for the better as well as for the worse. You might also work into your letter some discussion of Grandma's quote: 'We are members one of another' (page 152).

Comparing fiction and non-fiction texts

Fiction

In **DAZ 4 ZOE**, one of Robert Swindells's clear intentions is to warn readers about what might happen in a future society. Another writer who was similarly interested in warning future generations was George Orwell. He did this successfully in both **Animal Farm** and **1984**. He once said: 'Every line of serious work that I have written since 1936 has been written, directly or indirectly, against totalitarianism'. In other words, he feared how dictators could control other people's lives.

Read the following extract from Orwell's novel **1984**. It was published in 1948! In the imaginary vile society of **1984**:

- the Ministry of Truth spreads lying propaganda
- the Ministry of Peace is in charge of war
- the Ministry of Love tortures those who question the rules
- children are encouraged to spy on their parents

- a telescreen you can never turn off watches you in the streets and in your home

In the following passage Big Brother, in the shape of O'Brien, sets out to 're-educate' Winston – to teach him to accept that what the Party says is always true, by definition.

'Do you remember,' he went on, 'writing in your diary, "Freedom is the freedom to say that two plus two make four"?'

'Yes', said Winston.

O'Brien held up his left hand, its back towards Winston, with the thumb hidden and the four fingers extended.

'How many fingers am I holding up, Winston?'

'Four.'

'And if the Party says that it is not four but five – then how many?'

'Four.'

The word ended in a gasp of pain. The needle of the dial had shot up to fifty-five. The sweat had sprung out all over Winston's body. The air tore into his lungs and issued again in deep groans which even by clenching his teeth he could not stop. O'Brien watched him, the four fingers still extended. He drew back the lever. This time the pain was only slightly eased.

'How many fingers, Winston?'

The needle went up to sixty.

'How many fingers, Winston?'

'Four! Four! What else can I say? Four!'

The needle must have risen again, but he did not look at it. The heavy, stern face and the four fingers filled his vision. The fingers stood up before his eyes like pillars, enormous, blurry, and seeming to vibrate, but unmistakably four.

'How many fingers, Winston?'

'Four! Stop it, stop it! How can you go on? Four! Four!'

'How many fingers, Winston?'

'Five! Five! Five!'

'No, Winston, that is no use. You are lying. You still think there are four. How many fingers, please?'

'Four! Five! Four! Anything you like. Only stop it, stop the pain!'

Abruptly he was sitting up with O'Brien's arm round his shoulders. He had perhaps lost consciousness for a few seconds. The bonds that had held his body down were loosened. He felt very cold, he was shaking uncontrollably, his teeth were chattering, the tears were rolling down his cheeks. For a moment he clung to O'Brien like a baby, curiously comforted by the heavy arm round his shoulders. He had the feeling that O'Brien was his protector, that the pain was something that came from outside, from some other source, and that it was O'Brien who would save him from it.

'You are a slow learner, Winston,' said O'Brien gently.

'How can I help it?' he blubbered. 'How can I help seeing what is in front of my eyes? Two and two are four.'

'Sometimes, Winston. Sometimes they are five. Sometimes they are three. Sometimes they are all of them at once. You must try harder. It is not easy to become sane.'

He laid Winston down on the bed. The grip of his limbs tightened again, but the pain had ebbed away and the trembling had stopped, leaving him merely weak and cold. O'Brien motioned with his head to the man in the white coat, who had stood immobile throughout the proceedings. The man in the white coat bent down and looked closely into Winston's eyes, felt his pulse, laid an ear against his chest, tapped here and there; then he nodded to O'Brien.

'Again,' said O'Brien.

The pain flowed into Winston's body. The needle must be at seventy, seventy-five. He had shut his eyes this time. He knew that the fingers were still there, and still four. All that mattered was somehow to stay alive until the spasm was over. He had ceased to notice whether he was crying out or not. The pain lessened again. He opened his eyes. O'Brien had drawn back the lever.

'How many fingers, Winston?'

'Four. I suppose there are four. I would see five if I could. I am trying to see five.'

'Which do you wish: to persuade me that you see five, or really to see them?'

'Really to see them.'

'Again.' said O'Brien.

Perhaps the needle was at eighty – ninety. Winston could not intermittently remember why the pain was happening. Behind his screwed-up eyelids *a forest of fingers seemed to be moving in a sort of dance, weaving in and out, disappearing behind one another and reappearing again. He was trying to count them, he could not remember why. He knew only that it was impossible to count them, and that this was somehow due to the mysterious identity between five and four. The pain died down again. When he opened his eyes it was to find that he was still seeing the same thing. Innumerable fingers, like moving trees, were still streaming past in either direction, crossing and recrossing. He shut his eyes again.*

'How many fingers am I holding up, Winston?'

'I don't know. I don't know. You will kill me if you do that again. Four, five, six — in all honesty I don't know.'

'Better,' said O'Brien.

George Orwell, *1984* (Longman), pp. 42–4

(a) What is your reaction to this extract?
(b) What does it have in common with parts of **DAZ 4 ZOE**? Think of both ideas and style of writing.
(c) Do writers need to shock their readers in order to warn them?

Non-fiction

Read the following visions of what society in the twenty-first century might be like.

It is Friday, 28th December in the year 2029. The hour is 0808 EST (European Standard Time). Susan Smith checks this on her personal computer screen together with the local weather and traffic news, and her day's appointments.

Susan, born in the first hour of the first day of the first year of the 21st century, is a professional personal tutor to nineteen children aged from eight to ten years.

She tutors the children with their parents, or in small groups, in their homes, in her home, in community resource centres, in field stations, in museums and art galleries, in concert halls and theatres, in libraries and sports centres, and in other places where, in her professional opinion, advantage to her clients will accrue.

Susan is not a teacher in the 19th or 20th Century sense of the word. She does not teach in a school. There are no teachers and there are no schools. There are simply personal tutors, pupils, parents, and extensive support facilities.

Susan possesses, for each of the children in her tutorial group, a personal study programme. She devised each programme with the help of the child, his parents, and colleagues' notes on the child's earlier achievements. She did this before the child first came to her from his previous tutor at the age of eight. The programme outlines the child's studies for the next two years and Susan reviews it each month – again with the help and concurrence of the child's family. She calls on help from colleagues and such other support agencies as she feels are needed. She then sets a detailed study programme for the days immediately ahead.

Susan takes responsibility for the appropriateness of each on-going programme. This is her professional task: sound educational 'prescriptions' for her clients and the acceptance of full responsibility for the efficacy of what she prescribes.

John Adcock, **In Place of Schools** (New Education Press), 1994

The human brain may be connected directly to computers within the next 50 years, according to a far reaching study by one of Britain's leading technology 'futurologists'.

The study by Professor Peter Cochrane, the head of BT's high-tech laboratories at Martlesham Heath, Suffolk, predicts that by 2020 scientists will start to develop ways to link powerful silicon chips directly to the brain, possibly by growing nerve cells on the chip.

Such a link would allow someone to carry around the entire **Encyclopedia Britannica** on a chip inserted into their head. The link would create a physical connection between the carbon-based memory of the human brain and the silicon memory of the computer chip.

The link would hugely augment the power of a brain because by that stage silicon chips will match the brain's ability to store and retrieve information. Professor Cochrane's research suggests that should be possible by 2015.

The amount of digital information transmitted by optical fibres is doubling every year and the size of memory chips is increasing almost as fast.

This will create an ever-accelerating improvement in computer power, Professor Cochrane said.

'In 2015 the computer will be equal to you and me in terms of storing the stuff you and I can store,' he said.

Computer memories are growing so much 'very soon we will be able to put all 24 million volumes in the library of the US Congress in the living room,' he said.

The direct link between computer chips and the brain is the most startling conclusion of Professor Cochrane's study on technology trends. It also includes these predictions:

- *Daily health checks by computers over the phone by the year 2000.*

- *Automatic dialling by talking to a phone that can recognise individual voices by 2006.*

- *Artificial noses that can detect the entire array of odours identifiable to humans by 2008.*

- *Medical devices that can roam inside human blood vessels under their own power by 2011.*

- *Portable machines that can translate a simple conversation in two or more languages by 2011.*

Professor Cochrane said that past attempts to predict the future course of technology have suffered from being too conservative. 'My wristwatch wields more power than some 1970s mainframe computers. Ordinary cars today have more intelligence than the original lunar lander.'

The computers of 2015 that will match human brain power will be large supercomputers. Five years after that they will be desktop computers.

These computers will talk and listen to their owners, with apparent feeling.

Steve Connor, 'A silicon chip on your head',
Independent, 29 May 1995

(a) How do you see the future of schools?
(b) What new technologies do you think will change our lifestyle in a big way?
(c) Are cities likely to develop in the way **DAZ 4 ZOE** indicates?

- Write up your ideas in a short piece of autobiography titled: 'My lifestyle in 2040'.

- Compile an illustrated leaflet about how you imagine your own village, town or city will be when you are seventy. For example:

FACT	FICTION
– Cars are electric and only start when the owner's fingerprints are on the steering wheel. – All streets have video cameras	– Robots have replaced shopkeepers – Children attend Internet centres, not schools

Study questions

Many of the activities you have already completed will help you to answer the following questions. Before you begin to write, consider the following points about essay writing.

- Analyse what the question is asking. Do this by circling key words or phrases and numbering each part.

- Use each part of the question to 'brainstorm' ideas and references to the novel which you think are relevant to the answer.

- Decide on the order in which you are going to tackle the parts of the question. It may help you to draw a flow-diagram of the parts so that you can see which aspects of the question are linked.

- Organise your ideas and quotations into sections to fit your flow diagram. You can do this by placing notes in columns under relevant headings.

- Write a first draft of your essay. Do not concern yourself too much with paragraphing; just aim to get your ideas down on paper and do not be too critical of what you write.

- Redraft as many times as you need, ensuring all the time that
  - each paragraph addresses the question
  - each paragraph addresses a new part of the question, or at least develops a part
  - you have an opening and closing paragraph which are clear and linked to the question set
  - you have checked for spelling and other grammatical errors

1. 'troof is stronger than friction, rite?' (page 62). Is the divided city that Robert Swindells presents a realistic picture of the future? What is happening around you today that suggests it might or might not be?

2. Why are Daz and Zoe drawn to each other? To what extent are they attracted to one another because one is a Chippy and one is a Subby?

3. Write about the author's use of short chapters and 'cliff-hanging' endings to his chapters. Quote from the text to support your answer.

4. Discuss three incidents in the novel which bring out the stark differences between lives in Silverdale and Rawhampton.

5. Is **DAZ 4 ZOE** more than a classic love-story with a typical hero and heroine? Look carefully at how the author presents his two main characters.

6. How does the technique of using a double narrator help to give the novel pace and excitement? Answer with close reference to examples in the text.

7. Examine how successful the author is in getting his readers to 'climb inside the skin' of Daz and Zoe and see events from their points of view.

8 Characters in the novel have different ideas about:

- responsibility
- caring for others
- law and order
- the future

Compare the attitudes of two or three different characters towards each of these. Which of the characters do you sympathise with, and why?

9 'We are members one of another' (page 152). Discuss the author's treatment of this theme in *DAZ 4 ZOE*.

10 Discuss whether you think the novel is one that offers hope for the future, or is finally pessimistic. Answer with close reference to the text.

Suggestions for further reading

Books by Robert Swindells

Brother in the Land

This is the moving story of two brothers who survive a nuclear holocaust, told with the author's typical short chapters and lots of pace. There is very little hope for the future in this book and it offers a powerful warning about the evil of nuclear weapons.

A Serpent's Tooth

This is also on a nuclear theme, about a campaign against the dumping of nuclear waste. Thirteen-year-old Lucy is a strong central character who – like Daz and Zoe – breaks from her parents in order to achieve what she sets out to do. Thirty-five short chapters!

Stone Cold

In this novel the author pulls no punches, and tells it as it really is of homelessness on London's streets. The double-narrator technique is skilfully used: Link and Shelter have violent stories to reveal. This novel is recommended for comparison with *DAZ 4 ZOE*.

Other authors

Down and Out in Paris and London by George Orwell

This book describes very vividly the writer's own experiences living on the streets of capital cities. It brings home the desperate poverty that has long been a part of urban life for many citizens.

No Turning Back by Beverley Naidoo

Set in the 'new' South Africa, the central character is twelve-year-old Sipho who lives with street gangs on the streets of Johannesburg. It is very strong on the realities of life in today's urban environment.

Pig by Andrew Cowan

There are echoes of *DAZ 4 ZOE* in this novel, which focuses on the relationship between Danny and his Indian girlfriend Surinder. Urban poverty and racism are presented in a disturbing and witty narrative.

Come to Mecca by Farrukh Dhondy

A collection of stories about Asian and black youngsters in London. Their experiences of parents, school, cafés, discos and entering work are stylishly told with humour and a lovely eye and ear for the real world.

Across the Barricades by Joan Lingard

This is one in a celebrated series of novels about Protestant Sadie and Catholic Kevin. Set in Belfast, the story of their love and exile from families has echoes of Daz and Zoe. Lingard once memorably said: 'We inhabit only one body, but by reading and by writing we can live in many worlds'.

Wider reading assignments

1. From your reading of any of Robert Swindells's other books, what do his central characters have in common?

2. Compare how Swindells presents urban life in *Stone Cold* and *DAZ 4 ZOE*. Answer with close reference to the texts.

3. Think of Romeo and Juliet, Sadie and Kevin, Daz and Zoe. Why are writers especially attracted to love stories 'across barricades'?

4. From your reading of the above – or other – novels, what part does propaganda play in a good book? Is it possible for a writer both to educate and entertain at the same time?

Addison Wesley Longman Limited,
Edinburgh Gate, Harlow,
Essex, CM20 2JE, England
and Associated Companies throughout the world.

First published in Great Britain in 1990 by Hamish Hamilton Ltd
Copyright © 1990 by Robert Swindells
All rights reserved

Editorial material © Addison Wesley Longman 1996

This educational edition first published 1996

Editorial material set in 10/12 point Gill Sans
Produced by Longman Singapore Publishers (Pte) Ltd
Printed in Singapore

ISBN 0 582 30243 9
Third impression 1998

The publisher's policy is to use paper manufactured from sustainable forests.

Consultant: Geoff Barton

We are grateful to the following for permission to reproduce copyright material: Newspaper Publishing Plc for an extract from the article 'A silicon chip in your head' by Steve Connor from *The Indenpent* 20.5.96; the author's agent for an extract from *Nineteen Eighty Four* by George Orwell Copyright © The Estate of the late Sonia Bronwell Orwell and Martin Secker and Warburg Ltd.

Longman Literature
Series editor: Roy Blatchford

Short stories

Angelou, Goodison,
  Senior & Walker   *Quartet of Stories*   0 582 28730 8
Thomas Hardy   *The Wessex Tales*   0 582 25405 1
Susan Hill   *A Bit of Singing and Dancing*   0 582 09711 8
George Layton   *A Northern Childhood*   0 582 25404 3
                  Twisters: stories from other centuries   0 582 29253 0

Poetry

Five Modern Poets   edited by Barbara Bleiman   0 582 09713 4
Poems from Other Centuries   edited by Adrian Tissier   0 582 22585 X
Poems in my Earphone   collected by John Agard   0 582 22587 6
Poems One   edited by Celeste Flower   0 582 25400 0
Poems Two   edited by Paul Jordan & Julia Markus   0 582 25401 9
Voices of the Great War   edited by Geoff Barton   0 582 29248 4

Plays

Alan Ayckbourn   *Absent Friends*   0 582 30242 0
Ad de Bont   *Mirad. A Boy from Bosnia*   0 582 24949 X
Oliver Goldsmith   *She Stoops to Conquer*   0 582 25397 7
Henrik Ibsen   *Three plays: The Wild Duck, Ghosts and A Doll's House*   0 582 24948 1
Ben Jonson   *Volpone*   0 582 25408 6
Christopher Marlowe   *Doctor Faustus*   0 582 25409 4
Terence Rattigan   *The Winslow Boy*   0 582 06019 2
Jack Rosenthal   *Wide-Eyed and Legless*   0 582 24950 3
Willy Russell   *Educating Rita*   0 582 06013 3
                  Shirley Valentine   0 582 08173 4
Peter Shaffer   *Equus*   0 582 09712 6
                  The Royal Hunt of the Sun   0 582 06014 1
Bernard Shaw   *Androcles and the Lion*   0 582 29252 2
                  Arms and the Man   0 582 07785 0
                  The Devil's Disciple   0 582 25410 8
                  Pygmalion   0 582 06015 X
                  Saint Joan   0 582 07786 9
R B Sheridan   *The Rivals* and *The School for Scandal*   0 582 25396 9
J Webster   *The Duchess of Malfi*   0 582 28731 6
Oscar Wilde   *The Importance of Being Earnest*   0 582 07784 2

Other titles in the Longman Literature series are listed on pages ii and 195.